I0582951

DOG HOUSE

THE OFFICIAL NOVELISATION

WRITTEN BY CHRISTIAN FRANCIS
BASED ON THE SCREENPLAY BY DAN SCHAFFER

Copyright © 2025 Carnaby International.
All Rights Reserved.

This novelization is based on the original screenplay of *Doghouse*
written by Dan Schaffer. Novelization rights licensed by Echo On
Publications.

Doghouse and all related characters and elements are trademarks of and
© Carnaby International. All rights in the original motion picture are
owned by Carnaby International, and are used with permission where
applicable.

*Special thanks to Andrew Loveday from Carnaby International and
Soho Film Developments Ltd.*

* * *

The characters and events contained in these pages are fictitious. Any
similarity to real persons, living, dead, or undead, is purely coincidental
and not intended by the author.

No part of this book may be reproduced in any form or by any
electronic or mechanical means, including information storage and
retrieval systems, without permission in writing from the publisher,
except by a reviewer who may quote brief passages in a review.

* * *

echohorror.com

Contents

Prologue

The countryside sat quiet as the hazy summer day darkened into a moonlit night. As it did, and the sun settled behind the horizon, the temperature dropped. A typically English chill billowed through the trees. Unwanted and annoying after such a warm day.

At the back of the houses, an alley stretched between privet hedges and fence panels. It was filled with the houses' wheelie bins, as well as knee-high weeds. An alley that was usually more occupied by foxes than people.

But tonight, the foxes had run away, terrified.

Something far worse was here now.

Breaking the silence of the dusk, a uniformed man hurled himself down the alley, crashing against the fence as he tried to keep his balance. He was terrified and trying to maintain his breathing as he scrambled desperately. He was dressed in camouflage fatigues and wore a black beret, but these were not in as pristine condition as when he arrived. They were bloodied and torn, like the man inside. Large gouges beneath the rips seeped blood out in streams.

The shoulder straps of his uniform each bore a crown above two pips: a colonel's rank. He was a man of file and rank. A man of order. A man of plans. Now in his late sixties, he was a slightly overweight, sweaty officer, running for his life.

As the exhaustion kicked in, he stumbled against a fence panel. Panicked, he pushed himself back up with all the willpower he could muster. Leaving in his wake a smearing of bloody handprints on the slatted wood.

A few seconds later, something far smaller than him, and far more dangerous, followed his steps.

The silhouette the moon caught had the figure of a woman. Both graceful and sexy. But the creature casting it was neither. She was pallid. Mottled. Grotesque. And in each of her hands, she held long, surgical, steel scissors that glinted in the dim light. They swayed at her sides like razor-tipped pendulums.

They made that noise again. The same noise that had followed the colonel from the church.

Snip, snip.

Ahead, with no idea how close the thing was behind him, the colonel could see the treeline. They looked eerie and foreboding, but compared to what he was running from, anything else was preferred.

He didn't glance back until that sound got closer and closer.

Snip. Snip.

As he turned, he saw her in pursuit, staggering along the alley. Her scissors snipping at anything he passed.

Snip. Snip.

The scream the colonel let out surprised even him. He hadn't made a noise like that on either of his two tours of Iraq. Yet seeing this... woman? Or monster? Or whatever she was, rushing after him with a body of rotten flesh, gnawing yellowed teeth and those bloodied scissors... He could not keep his fear quiet.

He ran on. Straight into the treeline. Onto the darkness.

The woman. The Snipper... She came to a halt as she stared at the woods. She didn't follow. She didn't have to.

Snip. Snip.

Somewhere in the trees, the colonel screamed again. But this time it was not a surprising scream to him. It was warranted.

"Oh God! No. No!"

Then came the sounds of his deathly struggle. As bones broke, flesh and fabric tore. Meat was gutted and sinew snapped.

These were the sounds of the colonel's end.

A short distance away, in what had once been a small wooden doghouse, someone else was willing themselves to be elsewhere.

He was curled up in a foetal position upon the bare wood, wearing only sagging and stained Y-fronts. His body was pale, and he was shivering as he tried to keep silent.

As the colonels' screams rang from the trees, the man covered his ears, hoping to shield his mind from the current reality. But it didn't help. The gurgling screams were too close and too bloodcurdling to be ignored.

A few moments later, the chained-up dog, the one whose doghouse this man had usurped, was now choking itself on its chain, barking at something that had just entered its garden. This dog was a good boy. He was protecting his home. Fending off the strange thing that now stepped towards him.

The barks soon turned to pained yelps, then to nothing.

The man lay in the doghouse holding his breath still, as if that would work to get him out of this nightmare.

Outside, the silence was broken by footsteps hitting the patio slabs. Not bare, like the Snipper had.

These steps had heels. They clicked onto the concrete with unbalanced steps as they got closer.

As he slowly opened his eyes, from the man's low vantage inside the doghouse, he could see this thing's lower half. Long, slender legs in white hosiery, white stilettos, white long frilly wedding dress. She was a bride, but all had been shredded and stained with blood... and not her blood. In her lace-gloved hand, a long axe was held, scraping along the ground behind her. Fleshy, hairy, canine chunks clung to its blade.

The man could do nothing else but listen to her sickly and rasping breathing as this bride walked by. And as she did, he sighed quietly, relieved that she had not found him.

But she knew something was here.

As the sound of the boots stopped, she took a step backward, listening.

The man, barely able to think straight, did the only thing he could think of.

"Woof?" he said in a quiet, uncertain bark.

Of course, that was the worst thing he could've done.

The axe came crashing down through the doghouse roof. It split the wood with ease and narrowly missed the man.

He didn't wait. He flew out of the entrance before the axe could find him. But as he reached the grass, his foot immediately slipped upon something warm and rubbery. His heel had hit a long string of freshly gutted intestines, and sent him careening forward, hitting the ground face-first, slapping into gore that had once belonged to the now eviscerated dog.

Panic then outpaced dignity, as the man's bladder emptied.

He got to his feet, or rather flailed in that general direction, and ran away from the axe-wielding bride.

He sprinted for the back fence, the barrier he needed to put between him and the woman. But his legs didn't cooperate. After leaping as high as he could, he undershot the top of the fence by over two feet, slamming into the fence at full force, causing him to rebound down onto the lawn in a heap.

With a determination of someone who knew death

was at their heels, he hauled his sweaty, piss covered body up and raced over it, climbing it instead of stupidly leaping at it.

His remaining dignity was about to take another beating. As he landed on the other side of the fence, his wet, yellowing Y-fronts didn't. They had snagged on a nail at the top and stayed there, waving gently in the breeze at him.

Even though there was no one to judge, as old habits die hard, he cupped himself with both hands and carried on his escape.

The woods lay ahead, but he was not heading there. He was running down the alley towards the town, thighs slapping as he did. Out here, his full moon reflected more light than the actual moon did.

Approaching a junction leading left and right, he paused, thinking.

To his left came a sound. A moan. A guttural, horrible sound.

He did not need to hear any more. He turned right and ran, still looking behind him to make sure that whatever had moaned wasn't in pursuit.

Wrong move...

...there she was, waiting for him.

He didn't see her until the blades sliced through his cupped hands, slicing meat, nerves, and something far more vital.

His howls tore through the alley.

Snip, snip.

Lads F.C.

The clock radio alarm went off, slapping Vince in the face with its sound. From a grimy, half-broken speaker, an electric buzzing noise blared out that almost drowned out whatever Radio 1 had decided to pump out to their listeners. And on this morning, it was someone crooning about the female of the species being more deadly than the male.

Vince wouldn't disagree with that statement if he were fully awake. But at 8am, he was barely conscious.

His hand moved out from under the warm bedsheets and quickly went the wrong way, straight into last night's curry, all congealed and luminous on a plate, open to the elements next to the clock radio.

This didn't make him change course, as he hit the snooze button with a wet Masala smear.

As the room fell back into a comfortable silence, Vince sighed. Back to sleep and back to—

Not that lucky.

His mobile illuminated as it rang a midi version of *the A-Team* theme. Sounding wildly upbeat, it tore apart all serenity that Vince was hoping to dwell in.

He opened one sleep-crusted eye.

He was too old for living like this, he thought.

Yet here he was, mid-thirties, and clearly life had been overzealous with him. He was not what he once was. His blond hair had already given up the ghost, standing in retreating confusion around a forehead that grew bigger with each passing year.

In his youth, he knew ambition and adventure, but then life changed, and he began to know early nights, cups of tea, and Sunday trips to Halfords. He was happy with that. Fate had made him think that he was winning. Happy wife, happy life. But fate was also punching him repeatedly in the balls, and he had no idea that any of it was happening. He thought life was going beautifully.

Now he was here, a husk in underwear, sprawled on a single bed, surrounded by a battlefield of old pizza boxes, beer cans, and sadness.

He squinted at his phone, and as he saw the name *Neil* flashing on its screen, he turned it off with a grunt of annoyance, then threw the phone to the floor. He wasn't ready for the world or reality quite yet.

He rolled back into the detritus of his slumber. He needed to forget his failed life, and get lost in dreams for just a few moments longer.

. . .

By contrast, Neil was already vertical. Unfortunately, he was also airborne.

A stilettoed shoe collided with his face at speed, smacking him in the eye with a *crack* that sent him stumbling backwards, out of the door and onto the front lawn, wearing only his jeans and carrying his polo shirt and shoes in his arms.

Also in his mid-thirties, Neil was less of a husk than Vince, and was instead all swagger and smirk, the kind of man who would label himself Billy Big Bollocks, and no one would disagree. Loud, abrasive, and always laughing at his own jokes, he was the annoying sort that claimed women loved him, and was aggravatingly often right. His charm was the sort that only worked after five drinks and an apocalyptic lapse in judgement.

The woman on the doorstep, nearly a decade younger than him, was barely dressed in her underwear, and was incandescent with rage as she strode out, other stiletto in her hand, gripped like a dagger. She also carried a small wad of cash, which she hurled at him with a seething grunt.

"I'm not a bloody prostitute," she screamed.

Now standing in a flowerbed on the front lawn, Neil looked at her in confusion.

"Wait, you're not?" he asked, genuinely.

"This was our *second* date, Neil."

"Was it? Really?" He looked confused at her. "Look, love, I was on a fistful of tequila last night... What's your name again?"

She stared back, the shoe shaking in her grip. "You're kidding me," she gasped.

Neil looked her up and down, at her perfect body that was showing a bit too much for this time of day in this suburban neighbourhood. He grinned, despite the soreness of his eye, now swelling from a shoe hit.

"Y'know," he said with a cheeky grin. "If you *were* a prostitute, you'd be bloody minted."

That did it.

That was the straw that pushed her too far.

She lunged, and the second stiletto was hurled.

He bolted before it could collide with him, a half-dressed mass of confidence who then went to dive straight over the hedge, misjudged it, tripped and fell onto a grass verge.

Finding the whole situation funny, he turned back to the angry, yet stunning, woman in her underwear.

"It was a compliment!" he called back, before pulling the keys from his jeans and running over to his car, unlocking it. A pristine Nissan 350Z. A car that was bought only to impress himself. "I'll call ya next week!" he added.

As Elvis sang *You're the Devil in Disguise* from the stereo, his car skidded away, leaving tyre marks and any thought of dignity far behind.

Graham's kitchen was as sharp as his wardrobe, pristine white worktops, chrome edges, and all too costly to maintain. He stood in the middle of it, dressed like a catalogue model for asshole accountants who holiday in Milan, preparing to deliver extremely bad news. The news he had practised repeatedly since he woke up. He had wanted to say what his plans were for weeks now. But night after night, there was never a gap big enough to say anything. Now he was left having to explain just before he walked out the door, already with a duffle bag slung over his shoulder. A duffle bag that garishly stated *Lads F.C.* on its side. A bag that didn't match his look, this house, or anything else in Graham's life.

His boyfriend, Angus, stood at the sink, a cigarette dangling from his fingers, exhaling silently through his nose. The space between them could have refrigerated a pint of milk.

"Maybe 'Boys weekend' wasn't the best choice of words, okay?" Graham said apologetically.

"Whatever," Angus dismissed angrily. "Have a nice time."

"Don't make me into one of those guys who ditches his childhood mates for his girlfriend. It's for Vince. I'm so sorry it's last minute."

Angus rolled his eyes. "I don't *want* you to ditch your mates, Graham."

"Then what *do* you want from me? Blood?"

"An invite would have been nice," Angus replied, melodramatically.

With a resigned sigh, Graham pulled his duffle bag higher on his shoulder. He walked over, leaned in and kissed the air somewhere near Angus' cheek.

"No girls allowed, darling," he said with a smile, trying to lighten the mood.

It didn't quite land.

The door slammed behind him as he left.

Bex was doing *that* thing with her eyes again, narrowing them into a hateful glare and aiming them directly at Mikey's face. It was a familiar look, honed over years of arguments that always began with an explanation of '*It's just gonna be the lads*' and ended with Mikey sleeping in his car.

"That's exactly what you said about Neil's poker night last year," she groaned, arms folded, staring down at him from the porch as he tried to walk away, but the argument kept him pinned down. "Remember that, do you?"

"He didn't tell us he was bringing strippers. How was I supposed to know?" Mikey replied, attempting contrition but landing somewhere closer to a shit excuse. "And anyway, Neil's not in charge of this one, is he? I am. You can trust me!"

Mikey, though in his thirties, still looked boyish. But even that was starting to fade. His youthful face was currently under attack. Threatened by crow's feet and wrinkles that had started to encroach on his skin. He stood in a *Lads F.C.* t-shirt, gripping a matching duffle bag to Graham's. One that was filled with four packs of lager and a half-used can of Lynx Africa. He was a man who was prepared for little, but had a vacant smile, dreams of drinking too much and who failed to see the current problem.

"You're arranging this, are you?" Bex said blankly. "Well, that fills me with confidence, doesn't it?"

"We're not going to Amsterdam, we're going to my Nan's house... and I'll be back on Monday."

She shook her head. "I'll have all the locks changed before then."

She wasn't entirely joking.

Mikey adjusted the strap of his bag and tried again, this time with the weight of sentiment, which, coming from him, felt like a cat attempting to play a harmonica. "We're doing it for Vince, Bex. He's got me out of the shit so many times, I've lost count. He sorted me out when I came to London. I *owe* him. He *needs* this."

"He *needs* Moodley, does he?" she asked with a sneer.

Mikey shrugged. "Yeah, why not?"

Bex exhaled in a way that made it very clear she'd already heard this excuse from him, or variations of it, at least a dozen times in the last few months. "Lots of people get divorced, Mikey. He'll get over it."

"I know he'll get over it. Because he's going to spend the weekend getting trollied with his mates."

"Then why don't you celebrate your own divorce with him as well?" she said as she gripped the wedding ring on her finger, yanking at it. But it didn't budge.

She quickly licked her knuckle around the ring, not breaking her angry eye contact with him, giving it another go. Still stuck.

Mikey watched her wrestle with the ring, trying his

level best not to burst out laughing. It wasn't easy. But before he could mess this up anymore, the screech of tyres outside signalled salvation.

Graham's far-too-expensive car pulled up, radio thumping with a cheery beat.

Bex stopped trying to get the ring off and pointed at him.

"Michael, if you walk out that bloody gate..."

He walked out of the gate.

Turning, he gave a wave and a smile as if she was doing the same, instead of flipping him off and shouting obscenities like she was.

Inside the car, Graham didn't bother to look up from the driver's seat.

"I see your marriage is well into phase two, then," he dryly joked.

Mikey slung his bag onto the back seat and slumped into the passenger side. "Phase two? What's that then?"

"It's the beautiful part of any relationship. When the shagging like rabbits turns into fighting like rabid dogs... and all you have to look forward to is phase three, when you just stop talking to each other and live in a permanent state of 'what the fuck happened to my life.' Then phase four... You die."

Mikey chuckled, knowing Graham was far too close to the mark. "You spoke to Vince yet?"

"I tried. Couldn't get hold of him."

"Same here."

. . .

Vince stood on the first-floor balcony outside his small, depressing flat. Before he shut the door, he peered inside and felt sorry for the poor bastard who lived there, forgetting for a split second that it was him.

He went to close it, then opened. Then closed again. He took two steps forward. Paused and turned.

"What am I doing?" he mumbled. "I can't..."

He stepped back, then stopped. His expression formed a sneer, aimed at his own indecision. "Come on," he said.

He looked down at his hands as if they might offer a solution. They didn't, they just held his *Lads F.C.* duffle bag and his keys.

He opened the door again. Then closed it.

"Bollocks," he whispered. Because, of course he couldn't decide.

He remained utterly, entirely stuck between what he should do, what he was expected to do, and what he wanted to do.

Across town, someone else was in a similar state.

Patrick's house was drenched in the austerity of someone pretending the suburbs were some kind of grand prize, but to him, it was a symbol of how much he hated who he was. Once a corporate shark on the stock exchange, he had raked in the money, all while bankrupting others. All for the bottom line. All for his bank balance. And what did it get him? A house full of furniture that cost as much as a car, and a wife too spoiled with middle-class living to ever dream of changing it. And a feeling that he had lost his soul.

He had changed, though. He had quit his job only a few months ago, let his hair grow out, started wearing a Tibetan bead necklace, and finally *found* himself. Not in some ashram in India, but in the Hackney Community Centre, on a class about enlightenment and higher learning. The only reason his wife, Helen, endured any of this was because the money was still there. She also held onto a glimmer of hope that Patrick would change his mind and go back to the rat race. That this was a blip.

She stood in the hallway, a large glass of wine clasped in her hand like some kind of gavel. One she waved around in judgement at him.

"You don't know whether you're coming or going, do you!" she said, her voice halfway to unbearable shrill.

Patrick hovered near the door, caught between determination and confusion. He checked his pockets. Twice, then a third time. But found nothing.

His wife didn't pause for breath as she swigged her morning alcohol.

"The first weekend my parents visit in years, and you bugger off to the wilderness to rediscover your testicles!" she groaned. "As if it's not bad enough, I've got to tell them you quit your job to become a bloody new age hippy!"

As a panicked sweat started to take hold, his fingers finally found his iPod. Deep in his rear trouser pocket.

He quickly looped in his headphones and immediately pressed play, needing an immediate rescue from his wife's tirade. The soothing tones of a woman's voice slid into his ears like a sedative.

'Welcome to sonic stress therapy,' she said smoothly. *'Let's start the day with a smile.'*

He picked up a bag of golf clubs, as well as his *Lads F.C.* duffle, and turned to leave.

Beside him, a wine glass shattered against the doorframe in protest, as Helen screamed at him to pay attention to her, to take out the headphones.

He didn't flinch. He barely even noticed. He was already starting the day with a smile.

Back on the balcony, Vince still hadn't moved.

He stood with the bag at his feet, and one hand fiddling with his Zippo lighter. Snapping its metal lid open and closed.

Click-clack, click-clack, click-clack.

The flame never had a chance to ignite.

He then set it down on the low balcony wall that overlooked the car park and turned back towards his door. He hesitated, then turned back to the balcony wall again.

The lighter sat looking up at him. It was old, but it meant something, once. He didn't even smoke anymore. But he still carried it wherever he went. Embossed on its front: a single dog's paw design. A gift from his ex-wife. The only gift she ever gave him. He knew he had to get rid of it. To move on. But it was too difficult.

"It's a symbol of his identity and the source of his primeval inner strength," Matt explained, somewhat annoyed.

The shop hadn't made much money since the internet decided to ruin it. It was packed to the brim with shelves of action figures, above rows upon rows of plastic-sheathed comic books, filed in longboxes.

Sunlight bled weakly through the shop's dirty window, but barely managed to do more than create an indistinct glow from the outside.

Somewhere beneath the dust and the display cabinets, a carpet still existed. A threadbare excuse for one, that got even thinner every time Matt could bring himself to vacuum the place, which was not that often.

He stood behind his counter, wearing a t-shirt that said, 'My grandad was a priest in Trinidad'. An obscure quote from *Dawn of the Dead* that only three people in town would get, and he was two of them. He had the hunched posture of someone who'd spent a lifetime buried in comics, which, to be fair, he had. And like most of his friends, time hadn't been especially kind. Age was beginning to press in, but he wasn't going quietly. His hairline was holding its ground, though in true teenage-geek fashion, he still hadn't mastered how to style it. A stubborn tuft or two always stuck up, giving him the look of a man halfway to becoming a tramp. He was a relic of his own making, the product of years spent hiding in fantasy worlds while the real one aged him.

He was mid-sentence, trying to sell an *Evil Dead* comic to a boy who'd rolled in on a skateboard, who was now looking at him like a sad old man. The boy flipped through the comic idly, unconvinced.

"Okay," the boy said, half-bored. "If it's his inner strength, how come the zombie girls kick his arse on page four?"

"They're not zombies," Matt complained, too loudly. "They're deadites."

The kid raised an eyebrow, trying not to laugh. "Alright, calm down. It's only a comic."

Matt recoiled slightly, as if the words had physically stung his entire psyche. He couldn't have stopped his reply to this even if he'd tried.

"This isn't *only* a comic," he gasped. "It's a unique and often misunderstood art form. A carefully calibrated fusion of image and dialogue. A marriage of aesthetics and narrative structure."

The boy looked unimpressed.

"It's picture and prose, you get that, don't you?" Matt added, almost pleading for approval.

"You mean it's like the telly?"

Matt sighed, giving up the fight. "Look, do you want it or not?"

The boy shrugged, throwing the comic back onto the counter. "Nah. It's stupid. I prefer X-men."

Matt's expression flattened. "Fine. Piss off, then. We're shutting early."

19

"Why?" the boy asked, not threatened at all. "You got plans, do ya?" he added sarcastically.

"*Why*? Space-time anomaly, that's why."

The boy smirked. "You just want to be alone with your missus." He nodded to the full-sized Bride of Frankenstein mannequin propped up by the sci-fi section.

Without waiting for a comeback, the kid dropped his skateboard, jumped on, and pushed off the counter. The wheels clacked as he rolled to the door and quickly disappeared out.

"Little knob-end," Matt grunted.

He caught a glimpse of himself in the mirror above the counter. Another tuft of hair refused to behave. He flattened it with his hand, but it sprang right back up.

He sighed, defeated.

Vince was reaching to open his front door once more, having finally decided that he was not going anywhere, when he heard shouting coming towards him.

Before he could turn, two shadows came hurtling at him, all swinging bags and cackling jeers.

Graham and Mikey, grinning like schoolboys, grabbed him by the arms.

Vince resisted for a split second, then had no option but to give in. There was no fighting what was about to happen.

"Calm down, lads!" he said, his Scouse accent out in full force.

They hoisted him off the ground, yelling his name like they'd missed him for years. He tried to look annoyed, he really did, but it all crumbled fast. A laugh came bursting out of him, unwilling but real.

Outside the now-closed comic shop, as a sign hung on the door saying: '*Closed until Monday*', a solitary egg sailed through the air. It exploded against the window with a splatter of yolk and shell.

The boy on the skateboard was already disappearing down the pavement, triumphant in his pettiness, before the mess even started to drip down the glass.

Patrick's house was unnervingly silent, save for the *chink* of glass on glass.

Helen was sitting at the kitchen island, with a nearly empty bottle of Prosecco in front of her, dripping its last drops of it into her glass.

One bottle down, and it wasn't even 10am.

Her lips turned to a snarl.

"Bastard."

Bex had waited precisely long enough to see if Mikey would come back as he should, with his tail between his legs, offering apologies. Of course, he did not.

With his PlayStation under her arm, still warm from his session the night before, she walked down the drive to the wheelie bin. Dumping the console inside, cables and all, she smiled.

"Bastard," she said in victory.

Angus stood at the kitchen window, inhaling smoke from the latest in his procession of cigarettes. He looked tired, not just sad. Just *done*. Done with it all. Done with Graham.

He exhaled slowly, as though to make room for the single word he'd been holding in all morning.

"Bastard."

Neil's car roared away, the stereo speakers still pounding Elvis, as he laughed, his eyes on the rearview. Behind him, the woman, barefoot and furious, was screaming bloody murder as she ran after him.

As his car picked up speed and turned the corner, she pointlessly hurled her remaining stiletto with all her might. It sailed through the air and bounced on the tarmac.

"BASTAAAARD!"

The Road to Moodley

The pub was exactly how a pub should be. Old, worn, and wood panelled. Three years ago, it would have been heavy with a perma-cloud of cigarettes, but now, with the smoking ban enforced country-wide, places like this stank of two things: stale beer and sadness. Or as Neil called it, *'heritage musk'*.

Six of them had entered with wide-eyed purpose, carrying their identical duffle bags.

Patrick, setting down a bag of golf clubs, offered one of his earphones to Matt as they took their seats. Matt gave it a listen, heard the ambient music under the meditative self-help narrative, and wrinkled his nose. He looked at Patrick with a face like someone had handed him a glass of rancid bin juice.

Graham walked over from the bar, balancing five pints on a tray, and placed them on the table, handing each drink out.

Neil, meanwhile, wasn't paying attention. He hadn't

even noticed the drinks arrive. His gaze floated past Graham and locked, instinctively, onto the nearest woman in a low-cut top.

Mikey held up the glass he was handed in protest. "What the hell is this?" he said, motioning towards the half-pint measure.

Graham winked and produced a second half-pint, placing it in front of him next to the other.

Mikey didn't know if this was making it better or doubling the insult.

Later, Neil sauntered out of the gents just in time to catch a woman disappearing into the ladies. He slowed. Appreciated her for a second and walked on.

And it went the same an hour later.

Just after finishing his second pint, Neil strutted out of the toilets, making no effort to hide it as he blatantly checked out a woman who passed by. And that moment, like before, like their bladders were on timer, Graham was heading into the toilets and caught Neil in the act. He shook his head in mock offense.

"You're such a savage," Graham said.

Neil burst out laughing. "Bloody right I am!"

A moment later, Graham was being as much of a savage at the urinals. Standing beside a tall, dark, and stupidly handsome stranger, he could not help but cast a cheeky side-glance.

Meanwhile, buying a third round, Neil was working his charm on the barmaid.

As she was pouring a pint, he leaned across the counter with the same grin that many a woman had stupidly fallen for before, and said something unspeakably inappropriate.

Her jaw dropped.

The pint didn't.

It was hurled through the air, beer thrown from the glass, meant to hit Neil...

Now, Neil may have been on the path to drunkenness, and he may not have been able to control his mouth, but his reflexes were on point. He ducked just in time, missing the flying wash of alcohol. Which, instead, landed squarely on Matt, who had walked up to help carry the round.

The lads exploded with laughter as they saw this. Their glasses clanged on the table in what could only be described as a Viking toast.

Neil turned back to the barmaid, still with a grin on his face. "'Ere love, another pint please. I appear to have spilled mine." He winked. "While you're at it, get yourself a snifter, too."

The barmaid found herself suddenly smiling back. She had no idea why.

"Here, Vince!" Mikey said, lobbing something across the table.

Vince looked up just in time to catch the familiar shape of his Zippo, nearly taking it to the eye.

"You left that outside your house," Mikey explained.

Matt raised an eyebrow, ignoring the fact he was soaking in beer. "I thought you quit years ago?"

"I did," Vince replied without explanation, pocketing the lighter. Wishing it had stayed back on the balcony.

Neil wasn't paying much attention. He was busy looking around the pub. "Hold up fellas. We're a soldier down. Where's Banksy?"

"Late," Graham and Patrick answered as one, neither glancing up from their drinks.

"We shouldn't be surprised" Patrick added, almost fondly. "He's never on time for anything."

Neil leaned back in his chair. "He was on time for his wedding."

That earned a wave of laughter from the table.

Except for Mikey, who looked confused. "Why's that funny?"

"Because," Neil explained with a smile. "He showed up on time. She didn't show up at all."

Mikey smiled. "Lucky bastard. Wish that happened to me."

Vince gave him a look of disapproval.

"I'll call him," Patrick said, pulling out his phone.

Banksy ran out of his house.

He was flustered and already way behind schedule, as he tucked his shirt into his trousers with his free hand, a *Lads F.C.* duffle bag in the other. Being a larger-than-average man, even this small exertion made him pant and sweat.

He yanked open the door to his van. A van on which *Banks Electrical* was emblazoned in bold lettering along its side. The rest of the vehicle, though, was pure midlife crisis. With chrome alloys, tinted windows, and a state-of-the-art stereo system that probably cost more than he had spent on anything before, it was a statement, but not the one he intended.

He tossed the duffle bag into the passenger seat, ready to climb in, then paused.

He heard a sound.

His phone was ringing. Somewhere behind him.

He turned and bolted back to the front door, patting down his pockets as he reached the step.

His house keys. They were not in his pocket. He had only brought out the van key.

Swearing under his breath, he crouched and peered through the letterbox. There they were... his mobile, ringing loudly on the sideboard, next to his house keys.

"Shit it!" he groaned as he let his forehead rest against the door.

Patrick waited, the phone on loudspeaker as Banksy's voicemail picked up.

'Hi, this is Arnold Banks of Banks Electronics. I'm not available to take your call, please leave a message after the tone.'

Patrick didn't hesitate as he shouted. "Banksy. You're a wanker."

The others around the table, on cue, started to sing a chant like they were on the terraces.

♫ *"Who's the wanker... Who's the wanker... Who's the wanker... on the phone?"* ♫

Patrick hung up with a satisfied grin. "I think he'll get the message."

Mikey gestured to the golf bag beside Patrick's chair. "I did tell you there aren't any golf courses, didn't I?"

"That, my friend, is why I've got *this* bag." Patrick smiled, lifting his duffle bag. "You don't need a course."

He unzipped the top of the bag and revealed the contents: hundreds of golf balls, rattling like currency. The others leaned in to see.

"You're just going to hit them off into the woods?" Matt asked. "What is that, like... Zen golfing?"

"Zen bollocks is what it is," Neil snorted taking a glug of his pint.

"There's more to life than football, Mikey," Patrick explained. "All we need is the open air and an open space. Right, Vince?"

But Vince wasn't listening. He was somewhere else mentally, staring out of the pub window with an expression that didn't belong on a lads' weekend. He looked morose, dwelling on the reality they were now trying desperately to distract him from.

Graham shook his head. "I don't think your new-age golf therapy's going to work on Vince."

"Vince isn't like you, Pat," Mikey said. "He's a real man who likes the beautiful game. Not the rich wanker's game."

Neil slung an arm round Vince's shoulder, pulling him back to the moment, and squeezed him affectionately.

"You should have seen ol' Vince in his glory days," he said. "We used to call him *Fearless*. He'd step into the path of a charging bull to protect his mates and still buy the first round from his hospital bed. And I ain't talking fucking figuratively. He fuckin' did that!"

Vince smiled. "That was only because you picked up what was left of my wallet," he replied, a flicker of humour showing, though an unconvincing one.

"Show it to Mikey," Neil urged.

Reaching into his pocket, Vince tossed his wallet onto the table. The leather in the middle was torn. Mikey inspected it with reverence.

"Pamplona Bull Run, ninety-six," Vince said as his face brightened. "Neil screamed like a girl the whole time."

As Mikey turned the wallet over to see the other side, a small photograph slipped out of the leather and landed on the table.

A photo of Vince's now ex-wife.

As everyone saw it, the mood changed instantly. No one said a word as Vince picked it up, took the wallet back, and slid it back in.

He turned once again to the window, trying to focus his emotions. To make himself stop dwelling on what once was.

Across the street, in a greasy kebab takeaway, a woman was sharpening a long, thin knife. Her expression was blank, but her gaze found Vince's and held it. She didn't smile. Didn't blink. Just drew metal against stone, again and again.

Vince stared, transfixed, but he was not staring at her. He was merely staring out at anything.

"We should do it again," Neil's voice said somewhere behind him. "Mikey, you'd love it. Changes your whole outlook on life."

"Oh God," Graham said. "Not this speech again."

Matt threw on his best Neil impression, complete with raised eyebrow and arms folded like a self-help guru. "We all need to stare into the abyss at least once. Until we've faced death, we can never truly be alive."

"Glad to see you muppets were paying attention," Neil retorted.

He leaned nearer to Vince, clicking his fingers in front of his face. "Snap out of it. Today's the day you rediscover your inner bloke. You don't want to miss a single second."

"My inner bloke is just dandy, thanks," Vince replied, not quite looking away from the window, still staring at the kebab shop, where the woman had now gone back about her work.

"No, Vince. You are *not* dandy," Neil lectured. "You've lost your way. We *all* have. Me included. We're suffering from social gender anxiety."

Neil reached into his bag and pulled out a handful of large cigars. He shoved one into Vince's hand and began distributing the rest. Vince just slid his into his top pocket.

"Social gender anxiety? Is that a disease?" Mikey asked.

"No one knows, Mikey me ol' mucker," Neil said solemnly. "*That's* the problem. The second you try to figure it out, you're already doomed. But not you, Vince. We're bringing you right back. All for one, and one'll be pissed by the time we pass out."

Neil then struck a match, lighting his cigar with flair.

The barmaid glared from behind the pumps. "Oi! No smoking."

"What are you going to do?" Neil grinned. "We've got you outnumbered."

"Oh, I'm terrified." She replied sarcastically.

Neil then stood like General Patton, addressing the table like they were his troops, cigar gripped between his teeth. "Here's the plan. First thing we do out there, is piss up all the trees and mark our territory. That is non-negotiable... Then we find a boozer and drink until we forget how to speak. After that, we just communicate in grunts for the rest of the night like cave men... Until we eventually pass out in the woods. Any questions?"

But no one was really listening.

They were all looking past him, nudging each other.

A young blonde woman had entered the pub.

She stopped in front of Neil as he turned around.

"Nice outfit," he said, taking the cigar out of his mouth. "Can I talk you out of it?"

She ignored the line. "Are you Michael? I'm the driver."

All of them gawked.

She looked around expectantly, but there was no reply. They just stared like goldfish. "You want to see my driver's licence?" she asked.

Neil pointed across the table. "Mikey's the squirt on the end. I'm Neil. Now, more importantly, what's your name, babe?"

She looked unimpressed. "I can tell you now it's not 'babe'."

He grinned. "Is this going to be a long drive?"

"Looks like it's heading that way, doesn't it?"

Neil laughed, then he held his hand out to her. "Let's start again. I'm Neil."

"My name's Ruth."

She shook his hand, but as she did, he handed over a palm full of cash.

"From now on, it's Candy. Okay?"

"Ignore him, Ruth," Patrick said. "He's a throwback. He hasn't evolved properly. May never be able to."

She sighed wearily, pocketing the money. "Whatever, call me Candy, call me whatever you want."

Mikey's phone began to ring. The same obnoxious *A-Team* ringtone as Vince's.

"Do *not* answer it, Michael," Neil warned. "She'll have your nuts in a knot before we've even got on the bus."

Ruth scanned the room. "We're one short. Who's missing?"

. . .

Banksy was sweating before he even put the van key in the ignition.

The van coughed with a stubborn rattle. A depressing noise of a useless engine. A noise that made him question every choice he had made in the last year, including buying this broken down vehicle.

He tried again.

It spluttered.

A painful explosion of combustion followed by silence.

"Please, come on," he whispered, like maybe the van would take pity on him. "Please, please, please."

Then, miraculously, on the next turn, the engine let out a roar. Shaking its whole chassis like it had woken up angry. A stream of black exhaust fumes billowed into the air behind him.

Outside the pub, the others were emerging into daylight with the uneven swagger of men already half-cut.

Ruth led the way towards the minibus, which was no more than a battered box on wheels. Vince trailed behind, lost in his own thoughts.

Two teenage girls loitered by a nearby lamppost, chewing slowly on thick lengths of black liquorice.

As he passed them, Vince looked back over his shoulder. One of them opened her mouth wide and revealed the mangled, black pulp of chewed liquorice on her tongue. A dark slime clung to her teeth and lips.

Charming, he thought as he turned back and boarded the bus.

Vince took a seat near the front, keeping his hands low so no one could see, and slipped his wallet out again. He pulled out the photo of his wife, *ex-wife*, and stared longingly at her. There was nothing melodramatic about it. Just a quiet contemplation that made him feel better. She always made him feel better... before, anyway. Now it just hurt.

Behind him, Patrick was settling into his own form of therapy. He fitted the headphones into place and let the calm serenity of the meditative self-help wash over him.

'Forget all your worries,' said the female voice. *'It's going to be a beautiful day.'*

The minibus drifted away from the capital, weaving through the smog-stained asphalt of the industrial districts, past the factories that lay behind iron security gates, through the outlying middle-class suburbia, and finally onto the motorway.

Behind the wheel, Ruth paid no attention to who she was driving. She was so indifferent, it could've been livestock or a load of parcels.

From the back seat, Mikey's phone rang again.

"Turn it off!" Neil shouted from halfway up the bus. "Seriously, I'll punt it out the sunroof if it rings one more time."

"Anyone tried Banksy again?" Graham asked.

"Ah, don't worry, he'll show," Neil replied, unbothered. "He's like Mikey's missus. You can never shake him off." He glanced out the rear window to the motorway they had come up. "He's probably right behind us."

He wasn't.

Banksy's van sat motionless on the hard shoulder of the M25, its bonnet open wide. Steam poured out of it in long, pale puffs.

An AA truck had parked nose-to-nose in front of it, hazard lights flashing. A mechanic in a hi-vis jacket was hunched over the van's smoking engine.

"Well, it looks nice, mate," the mechanic said with a look of pity, "but it's a giant piece of crap."

"What?" Banksy looked insulted and very confused.

"In layman's terms, it's fucked," the mechanic shrugged, wiping his hands on a cloth.

"It can't be fucked. I've only had it five minutes... It cost ten grand!"

"Someone's already run the knackers off it," the mechanic said. "You can't fix that with a nice paint job... So you got a ten-grand lemon that looks pretty."

Banksy's expression sank to sadness, as he felt every bit a failure.

With the drinks they had pressing against their bladders,

the minibus was forced over at a small petrol station lay-by.

Ruth turned off the engine. "You all got five minutes," she called out.

"Piss break, lads," Vince said, leading the way off the bus.

Patrick didn't move, and he stared out of the window, removing his headphones.

"What are you listening to?" Graham asked as he walked by.

Neil leaned over the seat, grinning. "He's listening to one of those 'calm your tits' podcasts."

"It's not a podcast," Patrick snapped. "It's a meditation."

"Oh, right, sorry," Neil replied. "Is it the one where they tell you to visualise your best self in a glowing bubble?"

"At least I'm trying," Patrick said, quietly, putting the earbud back in. Then, after a second, took it out again. "How the hell do you know about the glowing bubble?"

Neil shrugged, "It's just filler, mate. Those wellness tits say that shit to everyone."

"Yeah, well, not everyone's trying not to put a belt around their neck in the garage, are they?"

That took Neil and Graham by surprise.

Neil cleared his throat. "Look, Pat, no one's having a go. I'm just... I'm just being a prick, you know? Banter."

Patrick nodded. "It's fine," he said.

. . .

Having left the motorway for a winding country road, the minibus crawled deeper into what appeared to be a place that should be called nowhere-by-the-nothing. There was nothing but fields. No petrol stations, no Little Chefs. Nothing familiar at all. And the further it went, the smaller everything got, even the roads themselves. Trees started pressing in on either side, edging closer with each mile nearer to the village of Moodley.

The summer sun had dulled behind some rain clouds, casting a gloom inside the minibus.

Ruth, bored of driving, had taken to glancing at her passengers in the rearview, judging them silently. But one in particular had caught her attention. Sat in the row behind, Vince looked despondent, having not moved for the past hour.

"You're the one who's getting divorced, aren't you?" she asked.

He turned his head, meeting her eyes in the mirror. "Oh, yeah, thanks for bringing it up. I almost forgot."

"There are worse things than divorce, you know?" she said. "Rape, murder... castration."

Vince shrugged. "I guess," he said. "So, what's your story, Ruth? You don't exactly fit the bus driver profile."

"I had a desk job. Didn't like it. Figured if I was going to be stuck in a box all day..."

"...It might as well have wheels," Vince finished.

That got the smallest smile out of her. Maybe, she thought, *maybe* this one wasn't a total wanker.

She changed the subject. "So, what's in a weird little village like Moodley that you can't find in London?"

"Mikey's nan lives there. We're staying at her place while she's away." He then raised an eyebrow. "What do you mean, weird little village? What's wrong with it?"

"It's just a dead end in the middle of the woods. There's nothing there," she explained. "When I saw the booking, I thought it was a wind-up."

Neil, overhearing (intentionally) from a few seats back, chimed in. "Mikey reckons the women outnumber the men there, four to one."

"Oh yeah?" Ruth replied with maximum sarcasm. "So, obviously they're all gagging for it, right?"

"Right," Neil replied, ignoring her tone, and just smiling back.

Ruth laughed. "An entire village full of man-hungry women just waiting to jump the first band of desperados that rolls up from London?"

"You've been there before then?" Neil teased.

"My firm hasn't booked a trip to Moodley in years," Ruth replied. "It's not a place you go to. It's a place you end up in."

"Well, for Lads F.C.," Neil said proudly, looking around his friends. "We are gonna take that little hamlet by storm, and rub our balls all over it! Am I right?"

Ruth furrowed her brow and turned her gaze in the mirror back to Vince. *Lads F.C.?* she mouthed silently.

He just shook his head to her. A motion that said both 'don't ask', and 'I'm sorry you have to be here listening to this.'

The moment her eyes went back to the road, her feet slammed on the brakes.

Tyres squealed against the tarmac as the minibus jerked to a stop, skidding sideways.

As it did, Patrick was pulled out of listening to his meditative guide.

The voice from his headphone persisted, cheerfully unaware, as Patrick went white with shock from the interruption.

'There is no cause for alarm. You are perfectly safe. Remain happy and you will have a pleasant day.'

The minibus had come to a complete stop on a narrow country lane lined with wilting hedgerows and foliage that was starting to encroach onto the road. The trees above knotted so tightly that the gloomy sun did little to light their way. The minibus headlights shone down the lane, reflecting off a thin mist that hung low ahead.

The six men stood in a vaguely confused line beside the vehicle. Ruth, with both hands on her hips, looked annoyed.

In front of them, lying in the road, were two sheep. Or what had, until very recently, been two sheep. Now they were just a pile of wool, blood, and steam that rose off their still warm and exposed entrails. Unspooling out of their bellies across the asphalt.

The men stared at the carnage, slack-jawed and

motionless. Their combined urban experience had not prepared them for any crisis like this.

"Welcome to the country," Neil nervously laughed.

Ruth shook her head and walked towards the animals. "I'll do it then, shall I?"

Grabbing one of the sheep by its hind legs, she began dragging it towards the verge. With all her strength, the effort was high, but the path was slow. Vince quickly joined her without saying a word. Between them, they shifted the second carcass to the side a lot quicker.

The others didn't help. They just stood together, choosing to interpret this moment as a chance for a bit of light chat.

"So," Graham said, "what *is* your Nan up to this weekend, Mikey?"

Mikey, always happy to speak, perked up. "She's off on a cruise while the builders are in."

Neil stared at him, taken aback. "Builders? What builders?"

Mikey shook his head. "Don't worry, we won't see 'em. They'll be gone by the time we roll out of the pub."

Neil frowned. "Yeah, but what about when they come back at the crack of dawn and start drilling holes in things?"

Hearing this, Vince looked up from the ditch where they'd moved the sheep, his hands flecked with blood. "She *does* know we're coming, doesn't she?" he asked.

Mikey hesitated with a nervous smile. "You what?"

Neil reached out and gave Mikey a brisk, dismissive

slap on the back of the head. "You bleedin' tosspot," he said rolling his eyes.

"She's gone for two weeks!" Mikey insisted. "I know where she leaves the key."

Graham let out a sighing laugh. "This just keeps getting better. I think I'll stay on the bus and wait for the return trip."

From the grass verge, Ruth, wiping the sheep blood off her hands with a tissue, turned to them. "Gentlemen, I am sorry to be the one to tell you," she said, "but you are all way past the point of no return."

She pushed aside a branch, revealing a rusted signpost, half-hidden by overgrown ivy. The lettering was old but still legible:

MOODLEY
1 mile.

Before anyone could respond, the cheerful blare of *the A-Team* ringtone broke the silence.

Neil growled, "For fuck's sake, Mikey."

"It's not me," Mikey protested, holding up empty hands.

They all fumbled for their phones.

It was Vince's.

He looked at the screen, then raised it to his ear with a cautious dread combined with a heartbreakingly helpless look.

Everyone saw and fell silent. They knew who this was. They knew they could not say a thing.

The atmosphere immediately darkened as Vince answered the call.

"Hello?"

That first word out of his mouth was full of hope. But as *she* spoke on the other end, everything seemed to sink... his shoulders, his expression, his will.

"Yes," he replied, trying not to sound as angry as he suddenly felt. "I told you I'd sign the papers, didn't—"

She cut him off. He bit his lip.

"No, the Solicitors always say that," he continued.

Her screaming was loud through the phone. The others couldn't make out all the words, but they could hear the rage now being unloaded on their friend.

"No. I can't do anything today... No, I'm not in London..."

And then, clear as day, the voice from the phone rang out for all to hear: '*Where the fuck are you*?'

"Moodley... Moodley!"

Her fury turned to cruel laughter.

"What do you mean it's a shit hole?"

By the time the line went dead, Vince looked like a shell of the man who had picked up the call.

"Hello?" he said weakly.

He slowly put the phone into his pocket without a word.

The group looked away politely, but the atmosphere had soured.

Then Mikey's phone started ringing again.

Neil didn't hesitate. He snatched the phone out of Mikey's hand mid-ring and hung up the call. Walking back into the minibus, he soon emerged with a duffel bag.

Throwing Mikey's phone inside, he held the open bag up to the rest of them.

"Ladies, I want no fuckin' palaver about this... Phones off and in the bag. Come on. Let's have 'em. Getting away from it all does *not* include any spousal abuse via T-Mobile. You understand?"

One by one, they complied. Graham tossed his in without a care. Patrick sighed, but followed suit. Matt didn't mind, no one ever called him anyway, and Vince... he hesitated, but knew that he could not take more calls like that. He dropped his phone in with a smile, trying to forget what just happened.

Ruth, still slightly blood-smeared and very much unimpressed, approached the minibus door.

Neil stood aside with an exaggerated bow to her. "Ladies first."

Ruth didn't flinch. "After you, then precious."

Arrival

The sun had begun to sink further, casting rays of rusty gold across the countryside leading to Moodley.

"Look at that arse," Neil exclaimed while pointing out of the window.

At the side of the road, next to a large welcome sign, a woman leaned over a fence, facing away from them. She looked like a calendar girl: high heels, short skirt, hair falling in waves down her back.

Most of the boys on the bus pressed their faces against the windows, gawking, aside from Graham, who just shook his head in dismay.

But as the bus passed the woman, no one inside could see what was really happening. The woman, doubled over the fence at the waist, was convulsing where she stood. From behind the veil of long curls came a spray of thick, black liquid from her mouth. Not vomit. Like oil, but thicker and bubbling. It hit the field in front of her in a sludgy burst, like some sort of fizzy treacle. And it kept coming. More and more spewed out, more than a stomach should be able to contain.

Moodley appeared in the windscreen with zero fanfare. It was just a road that suddenly wound into a car park overlooking the village. No slow drive through any suburbs. No industrial areas confined to the outskirts... It was just tree, field, tree, field, tree, field, Moodley.

The minibus came to a stop next to a small billboard opposite the entrance. It was not a feature that was expected here. A twenty-five-foot-high ad overlooking a tiny village seemed extremely out of place. On it was an advert for men's razors, but part of the poster had been torn to reveal the advert lurking underneath. One for tampons.

They all filed off the minibus slowly, stretching their limbs like they were on an overnight trip, not one for only a few hours.

Neil was the last to get off, and one look at the view and his face fell like an overcooked soufflé. He turned to Ruth. "Tell me you took a wrong turn, and this is a stop before we get there?"

She was already lighting a cigarette as she laughed. "Told you the place was dead."

Moodley had the feel of a town that had stopped evolving somewhere around 1975 and had just sat there since. What had, in days long gone, been a row of tidy bungalows now formed a small high street.

A toy store stood inexplicably protected by barred windows, as if criminals often travelled miles from anywhere to break in there and steal dolls or a railway set.

Next to it, the convenience store's sign hung down, *Moodley Mini-Mart*.

The hairdresser's called *Snippers* appeared ordinary enough, if you ignored the large, spiderwebbed crack across its window.

The women's clothing shop, *Fashion Victemmes*, was something else entirely. Its faded pink lettering looked like it was styled in tribute to the Spice Girls, and had no clue what fashion actually was.

Outside the old pub, a shopping trolley stood abandoned on the pavement, a torn box of detergent sat inside it, half-spilling its powder across the ground, whipped into a cloud as the breeze caught it.

The oddest sight by far was nestled among these provincial storefronts: a small occult store, as unexpected as it was unsettling.

At the far end of the village loomed an old church. Towering scaffolding wrapped around its steeple, in a mess of iron poles and green netting.

"Looks like the whole village's called the builders in," Graham said, "and buggered off with Mikey's nan."

No one laughed.

In all, it was a strange-looking town, but it was one that also appeared abandoned.

Apart from the minibus, the only other vehicle they

could see was a mud-splattered Range Rover parked across from them. There were no other cars.

As they all stared, wondering why they were here, no one saw the football tumble across the street. If they had, they might have noticed that one side was matted with something red and crusty.

Neil turned to Mikey with a condemning gaze, and Mikey just squirmed, offering a weak smile of apology.

Patrick, meanwhile, had walked over to a large Tourist Information Board that stood at the edge of the car park. A large red arrow on it pointed to a place that said *You Are Here*. Studying the map, Patrick soon saw that the arrow pointed to nothing discernible, surrounded on the map by nothing except fields and woodland.

"Guys, I found out where we are," he announced, looking back at them. "We're in the middle of fucking nowhere... I mean who has a fucking tourist board in a place the size of first-class stamp?"

Trying to force a good time, Mikey smiled. "Come on then lads, let's get to it." He stepped back onto the minibus to fetch his bag, but Neil stopped him with a hand on his shoulder.

"Oi, leave everything until we've done a bit of reconnaissance, okay?" Neil was not messing around. This was cutting seriously into his drinking and womanizing time, and he didn't appreciate any of this. "We might not be staying," he added.

Mikey looked upset. His big idea was coming apart at the seams. He turned to Ruth.

"You hangin' around?" he asked.

She was busily applying eyedrops. "I'm off the clock for half an hour," she said. "Then I'm leaving with or without you." She looked at him with increasingly red-rimmed eyes.

Mikey, feeling deflated, shuffled after the others as they walked from the car park, down into the village. But as he walked, he noticed the football on the grass verge.

Trying to restore some levity, he called out. "Neil! On your head, son!"

He kicked the ball.

Neil, however, wasn't interested. The ball sailed past his head and rolled off down a side street.

The pub sign swung lazily in the wind, letting out an arthritic whine that seemed like the soundtrack to the whole of Moodley.

The Cock and Bull.

Neil would have made an endless joke at that name. But he was too concerned with making sure it was open. As they got closer, they could see more clearly through the windows, at the faint glow of the bar lights.

"Thank bollocks for small mercies," Neil said, relieved.

Mikey stopped as they passed the Moodley Mini-Mart and squinted back up the street, then down again. "I'm sure this place used to be bigger."

"Drinks look sorted." Neil motioned to the pub. "Now, where's all the bloody women, then, Mikey?"

"Look, there's one." Matt pointed ahead.

They all turned to follow his finger, catching only a glimpse: the back of a woman disappearing behind a building halfway up the street. Heels, bare legs, skirt too short for weather like this. The same woman they passed earlier. Now gone before anyone could call after her.

Vince, caught off-guard by the ludicrousness of it all, let out a low chuckle.

Everyone turned to look at him.

Neil raised an eyebrow. "Misery loves company, eh?"

"When was the last time you were here, Mikey?" Vince laughed.

Mikey looked unsure. "Been a few years, I guess... Ten?"

Graham suddenly clapped his hands together. A loud *smack* that startled them. He took a step forward, assuming command.

"Right, well, there is no point swimmin' against a tide of shit... We're all here now. So, Mikey, you're goin' to break into your Nan's house or whatever you've got to do to find me a nice warm bed for the night. The rest of us are going to get the bevvied up in The Cock and Bollocks here, and drink until Moodley starts to look like Barbados. Agreed?"

Without waiting for approval, he turned to walk towards the pub.

The others followed with a shrug.

This band of friends was possibly the least observant group in the south of England. They had walked into

Moodley, obliviously. None of them had seen the blood on street signs or across windows. They had not questioned a thing they saw, as they all just trundled towards alcohol, presuming all small villages must be like this.

Graham called back before walking in. "Someone invite Candy down for a drink."

"I'll go," Neil and Matt both said.

Patrick walked back towards the minibus before either could turn. "I'll go. If she sees either of you coming, she's liable to drive off with all our stuff."

"What are you talking about?" Neil looked genuinely out off. "Women love me."

Matt grinned. "You're a long way from your Nissan, mate."

Approaching the abandoned shopping trolley, Matt grabbed it by the handles, and hopped onto the back, pushing himself forward along the pavement, near to the pub. It wobbled along with zero grace, dripping detergent from the split box as it went.

The Cock and Bull was dead.

Empty of anyone.

The lights were on, but it did not feel welcoming.

Vince sat on a stool, one foot resting on the lower rung. The other dangling.

From his pocket, he brought out his Zippo, and began flicking it open and shut again, the metal *click-clack* echoing loudly in this place. It fell in beat with the only other sound in here, the clock above the bar that ticked along.

Patrick and Neil stood behind him, staring at the beer pumps on offer.

"I'm going for a slash," Neil said. "Get me a pint of the usual."

Patrick stared at him as he walked off. "Oh, Neil," his words were dripping with sarcasm. "Please. No. put your money away. It's my shout."

Neil didn't respond. He was already weaving around the tables towards the toilet sign.

Matt was still outside. He had gotten distracted. Instead of walking into the pub, he had rolled the trolley past it, stopping outside the occult shop. The sign painted in its window read: *The Burning Witch.* The faded gold letters were above a display of fake skulls, old, leatherbound books, and a wealth of curios for sale.

"Oh, this is so cool," he said to himself, looking fascinated by it all.

His eyes drifted past the display and over to the wall beside it. On the old brick, an electoral campaign poster had been pasted up.

VOTE MEG NUT
KEEPING POLITICS CLEAN
Sponsored by Wundawash

He turned back to the shopping trolley. Inside, the

torn detergent box still leaked its powder onto the ground. He noticed the company branding on the side: Wundawash.

Finding it funny, he looked back at the poster. One of the corners had started to peel away, and beneath it was another poster.

Matt raised a hand and pulled at the corner. Meg Nut's poster peeled off with ease, and beneath it was the stern face of her rival:

VOTE REGINALD PAWSON

No sponsorship. No tag line. No colour. Just stark text and a black-and-white headshot.

Matt glanced around the street. He only now noticed that there were campaign posters everywhere. On bins. On signposts. In windows. Any of them with Pawson's face had been ripped, shredded, or pasted over with a poster for Meg Nut.

He didn't find it weird, even though it was. He just shrugged, having no real interest in the machinations of village politics. Instead, he turned back to the occult shop and peered into its dark window.

Unknown to him, in this shop, something moved in the shadows.

It made a sound that could not be heard from the outside: a long, ragged wheeze.

. . .

The front of Mikey's nan's house sat in the shadowy dusk that now settled over Moodley.

A tall ladder had been leaned against the porch. Beneath it, a collection of paint tins, brushes, and tools lay sprawled out. One of the paint cans had been knocked over and leaked its magnolia contents all over the lawn.

She's gonna kill those builders for that, Mikey thought, staring at the spill.

He approached the house with a nervous reverence. His nan was not one to be messed with, and his memories of this place were of her shouting at him for any infraction, as if it were the end of the world. She had taken him in after his parents died, raising him from the age of ten. For nearly eight years, he'd lived under her roof, having to obey her strict rules and quick temper.

Walking up to a flower bed, he crouched beside a squat garden gnome. Its pudgy, jovial face almost mocked him for being here, as he picked it up to grab the spare key underneath.

But there was no key. Only the outline of where one had been.

The men's toilets in the Cock and Bull had the same charm that any aged utilities would have. Zero. Old yellowing urinals lined the wall, all but one working. The rest with handwritten Out of Order signs taped onto them. The smell wasn't just offensive in here, it was also mouldy and damp.

Neil stood at the only working urinal, humming cheerfully to himself.

A sudden noise startled him, forcing his hum to stop, and threatening to mess up his aim. He regained control quickly and looked where that sound had come from. That wet, coughing spasm that was unmistakably female, from within the cubicle.

Shaking himself off and zipping up, he could not help but smile as his curiosity kicked in. "'ere love, you okay in there," he said with genuine concern. "You know you're in the bloke's pisser, don't ya?"

He bent over, just enough to peer under the cubicle door.

The sound came again. A retching of liquid, followed by something lumpy. More than bits of food. Something larger hit the toilet water.

He could not see the black, fizzing, oily treacle that was splashing up the inside of the porcelain among large, hairy chunks of gristle. Bits of something eaten and barely chewed.

"I'll just leave you to it," Neil said in a hushed, apologetic tone, leaving the toilets in a hurry.

Back at the bar, Vince was still on a stool, still flicking his Zippo. The repetition was almost soothing to him, as his thoughts dwelled on the sadness in his life.

Next to him, Patrick leaned over the bar for service. "Hello?" he called out.

There was no answer. Only the *click-clack* of the lighter and the *tick-tick* of the clock.

Graham walked up to the bar, speaking low so as not to be heard by the others, now at a table by the window. "We must've been off our heads to jump on one of Mikey's schemes, and without asking a single bloody question?"

Patrick didn't disagree. "Ah, but his heart's in the right place," he shrugged.

"Shame his head's up his arse," Neil added, reappearing, slightly paler than when he'd gone in. "Line 'em up then, Pat."

Patrick gestured broadly. "Do you see any staff?"

"Na, but I think I just met one honking up in the khazi. Patrick's " He smiled, reaching across the bar and scooping a handful of peanuts from a sticky bowl.

"Maybe they're all sick from something." Graham said with a look of disgust.

Neil thought for a moment before any peanuts went into his mouth. He let them all fall slowly back into the bowl. "Yeah, alright. Wasn't hungry anyway."

Patrick's nose wrinkled as he caught a waft of something foul.

"What's that horrible smell?"

"That's the stench of the smoking ban, mate," Neil said. "Leaving behind..."

"I know... heritage musk," Patrick sighed.

"Heritage *fuckin'* musk... Stale beer and piss. It's what happens when you kick out the puffers. The smell of England."

Patrick shook his head. "No, this is something else."

Behind the bar, hidden from their view, a body lay sprawled across the floor, tucked under one of the shelves. It was the barman. Or what remained of him. His insides had become outsides. His guts, bones, and muscles had been ripped out and now lay outside of the skin. It was just a mass of gore, with blood lying in congealed pools.

"Where the fuck has Matt got to?" Neil asked, looking around.

Matt had not gone far.

He was still outside The Burning Witch, having been there longer than he realised. The window display was fascinating to him. As well as the fake skulls and books, charms hung on frayed cords. Bottles with labels advertising various sex potions, revenge elixirs, and healing remedies for the mind, body, and soul. Even a mummified penis sat neatly inside a velvet-lined cigar box with a sign that said 'Lucky Wand' next to it. There were also old VHS tapes on display, but they were hardly occult. *The Viagra Spell, Stamina for Your Partner, Sex into Retirement.*

As he moved along the window, to see what else was on prominent display, something on the ground caught his eye. The last of the setting sun's light flickered off a brass object.

He looked down, and his eyes widened. A spent bullet casing.

He could not help but wonder, how that—

A sudden grip on his shoulder, and Matt let out a squeal that came out higher than anyone could have expected.

"Alright, calm down, you sound like a dolphin," Neil laughed.

"Idiot." Matt chided.

Neil turned to the window display.

"Hey, look at that!" he said, with a sudden grin on his face." It's a nob in a box."

Matt didn't dignify him with a response, as he saw that the rest of the group were now coming out of the pub.

"We not drinking?" he asked.

Neil shrugged. "Like the Marie Celeste in there. Complete with a puking bird."

Graham was last to leave the Cock and Bull. He caught up to Vince and handed him his Zippo. "Here, you left this on the bar."

Vince took the Zippo, but didn't answer as he stared down the street. "Looks like there's life on Mars after all," he said, motioning with his head.

A woman had emerged from a dark stairwell from the basement of the small sandwich shop. She moved slowly, and each step rang out on the cast-iron steps. She wore a large, hooded puffer coat. Hiding her face beneath.

Maybe if they had not had a few drinks earlier in the day, they would have felt that something wasn't right with her. Instead, they just stood and stared, finding her stumbling funny.

The garden gate creaked loudly as Mikey circled to the rear of his nan's house, pushing his way through the weeds that blocked the path. Seeing a second gnome below the kitchen window, a taller and much more smug-looking cousin of the first, Mikey crossed his fingers and looked up to the sky.

"Please, mate, do me a solid," he prayed, before lifting the gnome and looking underneath it. He felt his stomach drop as he saw nothing, until there it was. Taped to the bottom of the gnome itself. A small key.

"Thank you, Nan," he said happily.

As he stood up, with the sun almost gone, he felt an immense sense of nostalgia being here. He looked around, remembering this garden. The same garden he used to play in. He remembered getting over the neighbour's fence by climbing on his nan's large plant pots. A fence that now looked different, as a large smudge covered the top of it. At first, it just looked like mud. But the nearer he stepped, the more he saw that it was not so much smeared as spattered. It was red, and still wet, and in the middle of it, was a handprint. A bloody handprint.

Mikey stared, not knowing what to say or do.

Back by the shops, the Hooded Woman had reached the top of the iron stairwell coming up from the sandwich shop. She moved gracelessly. Shuffling like she was heavily sedated. Her steps dragged along the street. Veering left, then right, with little balance to her gait. She then turned, walking away from them.

"What's her problem?" Neil said with a disapproving face. "She's movin' like a pissed leper."

In the half-light, even with a few streetlights now turning on, it was difficult to see her clearly.

Graham squinted. "D'you think she's homeless?" he asked.

Neil wasn't convinced. "A hundred miles from London, and the only person we meet is gonna try and sell us the Big Issue? What are the chances of that?"

As if on cue, everyone except Neil began patting their pockets, checking for change. An automatic reaction from their urban conditioning.

Then the woman stopped.

She'd heard them.

Wavering slightly, she slowly turned around to look their way. Her face was still hidden beneath the shadow of her hood.

Then something else burst into the scene, a blur of rage out of a side alley.

It was a man dressed in camouflage overalls.

A soldier.

He ran full pelt right at the woman, slamming into her with such force that her body lifted off its already unbalanced feet, then landed crumpled on the street.

Vince wasn't having any of it. He took a step forward, shouting sharply. "Oi!"

The others were already moving.

But the soldier was not listening to them. He stood over her, arm raised. In his hand was a glint of steel. A knife. Ready to stab her.

There was no hesitation from Vince.

"Get off her, ya prick," he shouted as he broke into a furious sprint. Before the soldier could turn to see what was coming at him, Vince barrelled into his back, hard enough to knock the blade from his hand, sending it spinning through the air and landing in the shadows by the path.

But the man in uniform didn't fall easily. He moved fast. As Vince had collided with him, the man twisted, using Vince's own momentum against him. He grabbed Vince by the arm, yanked and sent him crashing to the ground.

Neil was next in. He didn't shout like Vince. He simply launched himself at the soldier, tackling him sideways, catching him off guard. They both hit the grass verge, rolling onto it.

"Wait!" the soldier yelled. "It's not what you think—"

Too late. Patrick and Graham piled in, followed by Matt, all fists flying, feet swinging with unpractised and indignant rage.

The soldier fought back. This wasn't some drunk pub brawl for him. He was trained, and landed punches. Clean, heavy punches. He swung a sharp elbow into Graham's ribs. Threw Patrick off with a turn of his hips. Kicked Neil straight between the legs with a solid steel-toe-capped boot, sending him bent double, groaning, clutching his groin.

Behind, none of them saw the hooded woman sit up.

She shuffled silently over to the fallen knife.

After seeing the handprint, Mikey stepped cautiously through the neighbour's gate into their back garden. With one careful step at a time, his eyes darted nervously around. Not sure what he was looking for. But he remembered his neighbour. The woman who used to bake him cakes.

"Is anyone here?" he said quietly. "Mrs Broughton? You alright?"

In front of him, the grass was no longer just grass. In this fading light, he couldn't tell that it was a mess of hacked-off limbs that littered the lawn: a human foot, chopped at the ankle, next to a bloody slipper. A chunk of torso, or perhaps a thigh. An arm. An arse. All in chopped-up pieces. All soaked in blood, sunken into the grass, masked in shadow.

Mikey's eyes followed those dark mounds towards a large doghouse. One with an axe stuck in its roof, wedged deep into the timber. And there beside it, was a woman in a wedding dress, on her haunches, facing away from him. The sounds of chewing were coming from her.

Mikey had trouble understanding what he was looking at.

Her dress had obviously once been white. A mass of

silk, lace, and delicate embroidery. Now it was torn, drenched in dark red. Her veil still fluttered faintly in the breeze, caught on her matted blonde hair below.

Under the blood and lace, her skin was swollen, pale and veined with purple lines. Her eyes were milky, and her lids sagged down.

At her feet were the remains of what was once a dog. But now, it no longer resembled one. It was just fur, bone, and meat. Pulled apart into hairy pieces. Pieces she now grabbed and chewed on. Staring out without blinking, she devoured it one mouthful at a time.

If Mikey had seen any of this, he would have run. But all he saw was a woman crouching away from him, in a weird dress, making slapping sounds with her mouth.

"Uh... Is this a joke or something?" he asked. "Did you mess up my Nan's fence?"

This bride stopped chewing and looked up.

Her mouth opened slowly, but there were no words, just bloody bubbles. Followed by a clot of chewed meat that slid out of her throat and onto the pile at her feet.

The knife came without warning. One second, the hooded woman was sprawled on the street; the next, she lunged at Neil with a sudden, jerking twitch.

He barely had time to react as the blade went straight through the palm of his hand.

He screamed, falling back, staring in stunned disbelief at the wound. Blood immediately welled up, dripping out of the hole in his hand, dripping down to the pavement. He turned towards the scuffle with the soldier, and gave a sharp kick to someone's back—he did not know who. A kick of desperation, as he stared back at the hooded woman, holding the bloody knife.

"Help!" he shouted.

The pile began to unravel. Graham rolled off the soldier first, confused. Patrick and Matt then got up, now seeing Neil's wound and his attacker.

Vince didn't stop though. He remained on top of the soldier, fists flying at him.

"Stop!" the soldier yelled. "Please, listen to me!"

But Vince wasn't hearing him. He was unloading a lot more than anger. He was now venting all the emotions he had bottled up.

Two more punches and the soldier was out like a light.

As he shut his eyes, Vince slowly stopped and looked up with a smug smile. That fell as he saw the hooded woman.

She was coming at them, knife in her flailing hand.

Vince quickly realized the mistake they had made.

"Whose side are we on again?" he asked his friends. But no one could answer.

Even though they could not see her face, she was close enough that they could hear that noise coming from her throat. The wet, bubbling gargle.

Then the sound got much louder, as a sudden flood of black vomit poured from her hood, splashing onto the pavement in front of them with a glugging rhythm. It flew out, fizzing and oily as it landed.

The group all stepped back as one, their expressions identical. Repulsed.

And then something slammed into her head.

An oversized garden gnome.

It struck the side of her skull with a ceramic crack, and the hooded woman collapsed to the ground immediately. The knife falling from her grasp.

Mikey stood there, trembling, knuckles still gripping onto the gnome's cracked base. He looked like he might throw up, or run, or cry, or laugh, all at once.

"Mikey!" Vince shouted. "What did you do?"

He didn't answer. He stepped nearer to the woman, crouched, and reached out a trembling hand. He took hold of the edge of her hood and pulled it back.

What was underneath wasn't a woman. Not anymore.

Her skin was deathly and bulbous, pulled loosely over her bones. Milky eyes stared unfocused within their saggy sockets. Her mouth hung open, with teeth like yellow tombstones sat in black gums.

Everyone took another involuntary step back.

Matt's voice was small. "What's wrong with her?"

Mikey didn't take his eyes off her as he replied. "What's wrong with *her*? You are seriously asking that? I've seen her in your shop, mate. She's the bloody Evil Dead, *that's* what's wrong with her. And she's not the only one. I just left one by Nan's house. It's fucked!"

Vince looked about. At first, he saw nothing, only the quiet village. Then movement came from the side street where Mikey had run from.

It was the blood-soaked bride.

She rounded the corner. Clear as day as she passed beneath the streetlamp. The shredding of her reddened wedding dress trailed behind her as she staggered towards them. And in both hands, she gripped the large axe.

From the building around, more figures then started to emerge, as if called to a battle.

The barmaid from the toilet cubicle came out of The Cock and Bull. She was a bleached blonde bombshell after forty years of gin, fags and bad decisions. She had makeup plastered on her veiny face that was so thick, it may as well have been Polyfilla. Her fake eyelashes hung off her drooping eyelids. In her hand, she held a bottle of Stella against the wall, then smashed it on the brick with one clean swing. Leaving the jagged neck as a weapon.

From The Burning Witch, the shop door crashed outward, as something stepped out. With a black dress, pale skin, heavy eyeliner, black hair, and one eye covered by an eyepatch, she looked like a giant goth witch. Something large and silver was being dragged behind her. A ceremonial sword, large enough to belong to a medieval knight. Its price tag flapped gently from its hilt. She said nothing, but from her mouth a long string of black bile leaked over her lips, spilling down her chin.

Vince stared at the approaching women. "Hey lads," he said quietly. "Let's all get back on the bus, shall we? Sound like a plan?"

Patrick nodded to the unconscious soldier. "What about Action Man here?"

"Bollocks," Vince whispered, as he walked over and helped Patrick pick up the man. They carried him between them as the group retreated up the street.

Bollocks

Neil was first to reach the minibus, his adrenaline pushing him faster than he thought he could move, especially with the pain throbbing in his hand. He was half-laughing, half-panicking as he threw himself up the steps, shouting urgently, "Candy. Start her up. We are getting the fuck out of Moodley now. We—!"

His words died in his throat as he almost fell back down the steps.

Behind the driver's seat, Ruth convulsed violently, writhing as if being shocked by thousands of volts. As she shook, black, fizzy goo erupted from her mouth, nose and ears, spraying across the width of the windscreen.

Neil retreated in disgust and terror, down to the bottom step, as the others caught up to him, forming a paralysed semicircle as they stared up at their driver.

The soldier still hanging between Patrick and Vince.

The horror of the transformation became

gruesomely mesmerising. Ruth's face undulated like worms were moving beneath her skin. Dark purple veins spread rapidly across her face, breaking out to the surface in a bulge, crawling over her features like roots. Her wide brown eyes started to cloud, as her iris clouded to sickly white.

Only Vince seemed unfazed. His voice was calm as he offered a helpful suggestion: "Let's go somewhere else, shall we?"

"Yeah," Neil replied, swallowing hard, stepping off the bus. "Okay. Where?"

Vince looked at Mikey. "How far's your Nan's house?"

But Mikey was too busy being transfixed by Ruth's spasmic metamorphosis.

Neil leaned in and hit the door's control knob. As he pressed it down, the door hissed loudly, the gears kicked in, and slammed the minibus door shut. Trapping her in.

"Mikey!" Vince shouted again, yanking on his arm. "Your Nan's house? Where?"

Mikey finally stirred from his trance. "It's... It's back there," he said, pointing down into the town. Down where silhouettes of the monstrous women were—the Bride, the Barmaid, and the Goth Witch—all shuffled about in the glow of the streetlamp, around the fallen body of the hooded one. Having lost their prey, they now wandered aimlessly.

Mikey swallowed, reconsidering their path. "We can take the scenic route behind the shops over there."

The alley he took them to lay squeezed between a

row of houses and Snippers. As they rushed towards the path, out of the view of the woman, Neil caught sight of the hairdresser's door. Plastered with faded images of 80s hairstyles.

"On the fuckin' sharp end of fashion here," he mumbled with a smirk.

But before they could make their escape, the salon's door swung open, replacing the aged photographs with a nightmarish vision. With a pair of long, lethal scissors in each hand, she snipped them rhythmically together.

Snip. Snip.

Snip. Snip.

No one waited around. All six bolted, trampling weeds, skidding on loose gravel, down the alley.

They ran through the twilight gloom, led by Mikey, into one of the gardens, its fence having been knocked down.

They all soon stumbled to an abrupt halt.

Mikey now saw what the lumps he had seen in this garden were. Body parts. Dozens of people's parts, all hacked to bits.

On the washing line above this mess, clothes fluttered drenched in blood. It was dark, but they could tell two things. One, that all the victims here were male, and two, it was all very recent.

Neil shook his head slowly. "I think I prefer our chances with the hairdresser."

"Me too," Vince nodded, adjusting the soldier's weight on his shoulder. "Let's go back."

Turning as one, they nearly screamed at the ghastly

tableau all had missed as they ran in. There, strung up on the wire fence by the end of the garden, was a soldier.

A colonel.

Displayed like a gory scarecrow.

His gut had been sliced open, with his entrails removed and looped around the metal fence, like the fleshy rope that held him up.

Vince and Patrick, losing their composure, accidentally dropped the Soldier, who landed head-first in the bloody grass.

Patrick covered his mouth, suppressing the urge to vomit, eyes watering from disgust.

Neil, always opportunistic, spotted a blood-slick gun holstered on the colonel's belt. He jabbed Mikey urgently. "Oi, get his gun."

But Mikey wasn't having any of that. "Bollocks, *you* get it."

Shocked by Mikey's rare defiance, Neil reluctantly reached for the firearm himself, his hand trembling, as his wounded hand was held upward to stop the bleeding from his wound.

As he got closer, the stench from the colonel's burst bowel hit his nose, forcing him to gag. His stomach churned violently as he pushed himself to grab the gun and pull it free from its holster, tendrils of intestine clinging to it as he pulled his hand away.

Suddenly, the colonel's blood-soaked lips parted. "It's empty..." he whispered in a wheeze.

"Jesus!" Neil shrieked, dropping the gun.

"What was that?" Patrick said. "Is he *alive*?"

Mikey stared up. "Oh, mate. That is not cool. Look at the state of him."

The colonel's eyes fluttered, breath rattling as he fought to speak. Blood seeped from every hole as he rasped out a warning.

"*Don't...go...into...the woods.*"

"What did you say?" Vince asked, not having paid enough attention.

Neil looked at his friends. "He said, 'Don't go into the bleedin' woods'."

"Why not?" Vince frowned. "What's in the woods?"

"Why are you asking *me*?" Neil snarled back.

Mikey looked past the colonel and stared at the dark cluster of trees behind. "Something in there must have unravelled the poor bastard."

All eyes followed Mikey's gaze into the treeline. All fell silent, trying to figure out what could be there. What could possibly be worse than what they had already seen.

Mikey picked up a chunk of wood from the lawn, and hurled it defiantly over the fence towards the trees.

"What's that supposed to do?" Neil asked.

Mikey shrugged. "Worth a go, right?"

Vince, fixated on the colonel, repeated his question more insistently. "Hey, what's in the woods, lad?"

"Everything...you're...afraid of," the colonel coughed.

Before anyone could think about this vague explanation, the chunk of wood Mikey had thrown was abruptly returned, smacking him squarely on the head.

"Shit!" he cried, falling back.

Despite his agony, the colonel's face twisted into a bizarre, rasping laugh. "You have... No idea..."

But his amusement didn't last.

All the six who stared at this eviscerated man screamed, as from behind him, an axe flew down and embedded itself brutally into the top of his head, splitting it open like ripe fruit.

The Bride's snarling face appeared from behind the now open skull, wrenching the axe free with a barbaric, sadistic glee.

Still screaming, the men ran, tripping and scrambling back across the lawn, through the blood-stained washing lines, scattering bras and pants behind them, towards Mikey's nan's house.

Vince and Patrick had picked up the soldier again, dragging him clumsily between them, holding onto whatever limb they could.

They crashed against Mikey's nan's front door, as behind them, three monstrous women were in a slow, shambling pursuit. The Bride, the Goth Witch and the Barmaid. Their feral snarls crying out behind them.

Mikey's trembling hand fumbled with the house key, as Neil abandoned subtlety, turned around and grabbed some of the builders' paint cans. He hurled them at the advancing horrors coming at them from the other garden.

Matt, overwhelmed with panic, wasn't helping; his jittery presence worsened Mikey's frantic attempts. "Please, come on, Mikey, hurry! Hurry! Hurry! Come on!" he shouted.

From out of the darkness of the nan's garden, the Snipper, with the two pairs of sharp scissors, rushed at Matt. She came dangerously close, but suddenly paused. Her eyes focused on Matt's eternally unruly tufts of hair that stuck up. She was momentarily fascinated.

Then, on pure instinct, she swiftly, expertly, lifted her scissors.

Snip.

The tuft of hair went tumbling to the ground.

She then raised her scissors at them in anger, ready to strike.

Vince, dropping one side of the soldier, took advantage, grabbing a large bucket of black watery emulsion. He hurled it towards the Snipper. The paint, narrowly missing Mikey, coated her like oil, rendering her face even more horrifying.

Finally, Mikey's key turned in the lock, and the door swung open. They all pushed inside, hoping for some safety. As he passed, Patrick lifted his leg and booted the Snipper backward, now temporarily blinded by the paint.

They raced inside the hallway, Patrick dragging the still-unconscious soldier awkwardly across the threshold. The door slammed shut behind them, echoing around them like a rifle shot. For what seemed like minutes, they stood in silence, frozen in the hallway. Holding their breaths, bracing for an expected barrage of blows against the door.

But the attack never came.

Graham, with curiosity overcoming caution,

crouched at the front door and gently lifted the letterbox flap, peering outside. Through the slit he saw the Bride, the Barmaid and the Goth Witch storming off in frustration, throwing tantrums and their weapons alike as they went. Trailing behind was the Snipper, scissors snipping at empty air, as she stared through her newly painted face. None of them realized that they had run into a house. Their rotten and dead brains not having the capacity to realize such a thing. If it wasn't in front of them, they had no idea.

"They're moving away," Graham whispered in surprise. "I'm not sure they understand how doors work."

Matt thought. "Hey, maybe they're like vampires and can't enter houses without an invitation?"

Vince looked shaken. "Alright, you funny cunts! How is this supposed to cheer me up, then?"

The living room was a stark reminder of Mikey's earlier mistake in insisting they come here. The building wasn't just being redecorated; it was being totally renovated. Every room was a mess of exposed floorboards, stripped wallpaper, and piles of building supplies.

His nan's possessions were covered with protective plastic sheets. One of which had been removed as Neil stood by the sideboard, holding the receiver of an antique rotary phone.

"All the phones are fucked," he announced, slamming the receiver onto the cradle. "Bollocks."

Mikey seized the moment, unable to resist a dig. "'Let's put all the mobiles in a bag.' That was a great idea, Neil."

Neil closed the distance between them fast, his anger bubbling as he invaded Mikey's personal space and stood far too close. "Do you want to chat about this some more, Michael? I *love* to chat things through."

"No." Mikey's bravado fell at the threat, his gaze falling to the exposed floorboards.

Graham rolled his eyes at Neil's peacocking. "Instead of being dickheads, why don't we all talk about the unliveable state of this house we're supposed to be staying in?"

Patrick strolled in from the kitchen, breaking the rising tension effortlessly. "Back doors locked. Kettle's on," he said, as casually as if they were just round for some Sunday lunch. He tossed Neil a tea towel, which Neil gratefully grabbed.

He started wrapping it around his still-painful hand, peering through a gap in the curtains. "Well, good news is they seemed to have fucked off," he said. "I don't think they're coming back."

Click-clack.

Graham eyed Vince, who was by the door, back to nervously clicking his Zippo lighter. "So, what's going on here, Vince? You got any thoughts?"

Click-clack.

Vince glanced up, shocked to find all eyes had now turned to him, expectant, waiting for answers that he clearly didn't have. He hesitated, mouth open, but found nothing to actually say.

Patrick, ever the rational one, tried his best guess. "Could be a chemical spillage. One of the streams might be polluted?"

Click-clack.

Matt scoffed openly. "When was the last time you saw pollution turn anyone into an axe murderer? It's got to be some kind of genetically enhanced super-virus."

Everyone turned to Matt incredulously, but it wasn't a joke. He was deadly serious.

Click-clack.

"Will you give that fucking lighter a rest," Neil moaned. "You're doing my bloody nut in."

Vince paused mid-click, sighing.

"*Thank* you," Neil said.

Vince thought for a second, forcing his head back in the game. "Ruth didn't even get off the bus, and she *still* turned into that..." He searched briefly for the word he needed to explain, but gave up even trying. "Whatever it is, it's flying around."

"Airborne," Graham added. "In the air."

Mikey frowned thoughtfully. "Why haven't we caught it then? And what about him?" He gestured towards the soldier, still slumped unconscious in an armchair like a pile of dirty clothes.

Patrick offered a hesitant suggestion. "Maybe... only women get it?"

"What kind of virus only affects women?" Graham scoffed patronisingly.

Silence filled the room again, as they all thought, until Neil broke it with impeccable timing and a deadpan face.

"I know... Birdflu."

Laughter broke out like a nervous flood, spreading until all of them caught the contagious giggles.

Matt's question cut through, killing the laughter in its tracks, sobering them instantly. "So, where did all the men go?"

The silence returned, but was soon broken by a faint tapping at the window. One that drew Neil's attention.

Carefully, he stepped over to the window and gingerly peered through the curtains. He couldn't see a thing.

The tapping continued.

"Careful," Vince said.

Cautiously, Neil pulled the curtains open. Nothing.

He then eased the window open to get a better look.

Still, there were no monsters.

Before he could close the window, with a sudden fluttering, a crow burst through the gap, wings beating frantically against Neil's face.

He hopped back, blindly punching at the feathers and beak until, with a swift and ruthless snap, the soldier's hand appeared from nowhere, grabbing the bird and breaking its neck in one expert movement.

The soldier, now on his feet, scowled at Neil. "What are you, retarded?" He tossed the bird's corpse out the window, walked over and slammed it shut it.

Neil was covered in feathers, humiliated.

"You want to know where all the men are? I can tell you." The soldier's tone was grim. "The men are all *dead*."

Vince seized a poker from the fireplace, and gripped it threateningly at the soldier. "Oi, sit down, Andy McNabb."

"Easy," the man responded, raising his hands placatingly. "I'm not the enemy here, now, am I? You've seen the enemy."

"Really?" Vince said, still pointing the poker at him. "See, I reckon you're probably the enemy. You guys are always the ones who fuck things up."

Matt leaned nearer to the soldier. "Spill the beans then. It's a biological weapon gone out of control, isn't it? A super-virus."

"It's classified is what it is," the soldier replied.

"It's hardly classified now, mate," Neil said. "It's running around out there in stilettoes and a hefty want to murder us."

Vince tightened his grip on the poker and stepped nearer. "I said, *sit down*." He was not playing games.

But the soldier was not even slightly threatened. "Or what, exactly?"

The atmosphere changed in a second.

Neil and Graham lunged, dragging the soldier back into the armchair, wrestling him into submission. The soldier fought back, landing a solid punch on Neil's jaw.

It was all about to escalate further when—

"Oi!" Patrick's shout stopped them in mid-brawl. He

peered in from the kitchen doorway, face utterly calm despite the fight before him. "Tea's up."

The kitchen was as unfinished as the rest of the house. Bare floorboards, wallpaper freshly peeled off, paint stains on the metal sink, and an old box of Wundawash detergent sat on top of the nearby washing machine.

At least there were teabags and milk in the fridge.

The six of them, along with the soldier, were gathered tightly around the cramped dining table, finding a surreal solace in the mundane comfort of tea and Mikey's nan's premium selection of biscuits.

Vince sat opposite the soldier, staring him down with a wary suspicion. The others hovered around like vaguely incompetent henchmen, anxious but desperate for answers. Patrick handed the soldier a steaming mug of tea with a polite smile.

Neil slapped Mikey's eager hand away from the last chocolate biscuit, claiming it triumphantly for himself.

"What's your name?" Vince asked the soldier, showing no emotion.

"Sergeant Gavin Wright," he replied evenly.

Neil, unimpressed by military formality, and a mouth full of biscuit, cut in. "We don't give a monkeys about your rank. We just want an explanation."

"It's a virus," Gavin sighed.

Vince didn't miss a beat. "And why aren't we infected?"

"You've all figured this out already," he said,

exasperation edging into his voice. "Only women can get it."

"Why?" Vince asked.

"Just luck?" Gavin shrugged.

"That's not funny, you prick," Vince said. "Can you cure it?"

Gavin replied with very little concern. "I don't think anyone survived long enough to try, but that's not my department. I'm just here to do my job and put them down."

Vince pushed harder. "How did it—"

"Look," Gavin cut him off. "The only questions you need to ask are 'How many are there?' and 'Are they in our way?' This isn't a fucking adventure game. It's actual life or death. Us or them. The why of it means less than fuck all."

"How many are there?" Graham asked, taking a sip of his tea.

"The whole village has gone over to the dark side," the soldier explained, also sipping occasionally from his mug. "Most of them are out there in the woods, so if you're thinking of hiking out of here, better think again. You'll get your assholes pulled through your mouth holes."

"But," Patrick added, unable to suppress his curiosity. "*What* are they doing in the woods?"

Gavin shrugged, clearly not caring. "Maybe they're all taking a shit with the bears. You know how women like to go to the bogs together." He sighed, then shook his head. "Come on, you can't be that dumb. What do you *think* they're doing?" He paused dramatically, before continuing dryly, "They're looking for fresh meat. They got all the town. They are spreading out to find more."

"Hey, if you really are a Sergeant, where are your stripes?" Patrick asked.

Gavin didn't answer, just looked up at him coldly.

Matt jumped in to offer an answer instead. "He won't answer that. It's a black ops, right? You're off the radar. I bet nobody up the chain even knows what's happened here yet, which is just as well because the minute they find out that one of their science projects is loose, they'll probably drop a bomb on us. Am I right?"

Gavin looked wearily at him. "You've seen too many films."

"Yeah, but is he *right*?" Vince fixed Gavin with a hard stare.

"Everything except the bomb part.... Only the yanks do that."

Vince smiled. They were finally getting somewhere. "So, what's the exit plan, then?"

"Same as yours," Gavin said, putting his mug down on a side table. "Get on the minibus and fuck off back out the way you came in."

Mikey chimed in, chewing on a rich tea biscuit. "There's a slight glitch in that plan, Marvin. Bad Candy lives on the bus, and she's not accepting visitors due to a bit of a skin complaint."

"First, it's *Gavin*, not Marvin. Second, there are seven of us. As long as we avoid the others, we can take her on easy. I've taken out loads of them on my own."

Neil's eyes widened. "We can't kill Candy!"

"Right." Gavin said, sarcastically. "Obviously, she's much better off living as a spaced-out, psychotic zombie."

"We are *not* doing that," Neil said stubbornly. "Think of anything else."

"Alright, we can coax her out."

"How are we gonna do that?" Vince asked.

A smile crept up Gavin's face. "Easy... I know what she wants."

Night had fully taken hold when the group re-emerged onto Moodley's desolate streets. Gavin quickly raised a fist, signalling them to halt. An army command that nobody else understood. They stopped anyway, more out of confused obedience than military precision.

Ahead of them, the hooded woman could be seen, staggering into view.

"So there are three we know of," Graham whispered to Patrick. "Hood over there, the one with the eyepatch, and the one in the wedding dress."

Patrick shook his head. "There's that barmaid as well."

"Four then, so how many do we think are in the woods?"

Patrick thought for a moment, looking around. "Let's say there are fifty houses in the town. One woman in each, by average? I'd say approximately another forty-six then?"

Graham wished he had never asked.

Hood didn't notice them approaching and walked around the corner, vanishing from view.

The group moved cautiously, hugging the shadowy cover of buildings, careful to avoid drawing any attention from the zombies.

Getting to the edge of the car park, they crouched behind a low wall. Popping their heads up intermittently, looking like frightened meerkats.

When satisfied the coast was clear, Vince turned to Neil. "The second she's off the bus, start running like hell, and don't stop until you hear us honk the horn. We'll pick you up, understand?"

Neil swallowed nervously. "Why are you all so sure she's going to follow me?"

As one, the group answered, "Women love you."

Gavin grabbed the poker that Vince was clutching and handed it to Neil. "If you have to kill her, just do it. She's not Candy anymore."

"She never was," Neil said as his expression saddened. "Her name's Ruth."

Gavin replied dismissively. "Ruth? Candy? Whatever. She's a man-eater now... Literally."

Neil was not letting it drop. "Just *don't* call her Candy again, you get—"

"Neil, now's not a good time for you to suddenly stop objectifying women." Graham interrupted. "Be a new man tomorrow. Today, you've got to be that misogynist arsehole we all know and love. So get up there and get her off the bus."

"You know, Graham, with only girls getting this virus," Neil said with a smile. "You could get it next."

Graham cuffed him roughly around the head.

"Ah, you even hit like a girl," Neil laughed.

Graham smacked him again, harder, then shoved Neil out from behind the wall into the open street.

Neil fell forward awkwardly, poker in hand, regaining his balance.

"Prick," he whispered back to Graham, who just shooed him on with his hand.

Resigning himself to it being too late to back out now, Neil crept cautiously towards the minibus, which was sitting in the middle of the car park.

His heart pounded as he got closer. Peering around as he went, making sure none of the horde were in pursuit, or about to run up behind him.

Getting to the minibus door, he couldn't see much through the glass. It was dripping with the black matter that Ruth had vomited up on the inside.

"You can do this," he whispered to himself. Jabbed the 'open door' button before he had a chance to chicken out.

The door started to hiss and crack open.

"Nope," he quickly blurted, pressing the button again. Closing the door.

He took a breath. Nervous.

He closed his eyes for a moment.

"Fuck it."

He pressed the button again.

The door hissed open, and as it did, there, hunched

grotesquely in the driver's seat, was Bad Candy. She was uglier and bloated, snarling and twitching, but remained in her seat.

Neil gulped. "Come on then, darlin'." He said nervously. "Come and have a nibble... You know you want it." He timidly lifted the poker, leaned up the steps, and jabbed it at her side.

Instantly, and with incredible speed and strength, she lunged, snatching the poker out of his hands.

"Oh, bollocks," he whimpered.

Bad Candy was not stuck in her seat. She had been waiting. And now, she was finally ready to play as she leapt out towards him.

Neil lost his nerve entirely, turned tail, and sprinted desperately away, with Bad Candy in terrifying pursuit.

Her step was unsure and unstable, but she was still fast.

The rest of the group didn't wait as they had made it around the car park, and with Bad Candy off after Neil, they dashed towards the vacant minibus.

Gavin jumped into the driver's seat, fumbling with the keys.

"C'mon," Vince shouted. "Floor it!"

Snip-snip.

Slowly, everyone turned to see the Snipper grinning at them from the back seat, her face gleaming madly beneath the now-smeared black paint that had been thrown at her.

Snip-snip.

Then, without warning, the Bride sat upright, directly behind Mikey. Axe in hand.

Panic erupted.

They scrambled wildly for the door.

"Someone get the phones!" Vince shouted.

Patrick grabbed the duffel bag stuffed with mobiles, but as he pulled it out, it snagged stubbornly on something behind him.

Or some*one*.

The Bride clung to the bag's handle.

There they were Patrick and the zombie bride, starting at each other.

Patrick then pulled on the bag as hard as he could. Summoning all his strength. Every last drop... until... he lost. The handle was ripped off in his hand, and he was left staring helplessly as the Bride took the bag and dropped it to the floor.

He had no idea what to do.

Well, he had one stupid idea.

"Look over there!" he shouted pointing behind her.

A few moments later, Patrick fell backwards from the minibus door, clutching desperately at the bag of phones. He laughed as he landed on the concrete, not believing his stupid idea worked.

Upside-down and dazed, he caught a blurry glimpse of his friends scattering down the street like terrified rabbits. Then something huge blotted out his view, the

Bride, now looming above him, axe raised. Ready to strike.

Patrick managed to roll sideways just as the blade came down, cleaving a deep scar into the ground, only inches from his skull.

Getting to his feet, he bolted blindly towards the closest point of escape: a ladder leading down from the nearby billboard.

Of course, nothing ever went smoothly for Patrick. As he got to the billboard, the ladder was just out of reach by a few inches. Without any other choice, he launched himself upward with a desperate energy, managing to grasp the lowest rung. His relief of holding onto it lasted all of a heartbeat before he felt the Bride's axe cut viciously into his calf, slicing through muscle and grinding against bone.

Screaming through his clenched teeth, Patrick managed to summon all the panicked strength he had and haul himself up towards the billboard platform. Climbing one rung at a time, bag still in hand, as agony shot through every single one of his nerve endings.

As he got to the top of the ladder, he grabbed wildly at a railing for support, but its rotten wood snapped uselessly in his grip, sending him sprawling face-first onto the platform, broken wood in his hand.

Blood, Pus & Golf Balls

Neil was racing towards the south end of Moodley, Bad Candy at his heels.

"I love it when a plan comes together!" he shouted with a laugh.

As he vanished around the corner, two figures came out onto the street, riled by the noise. A zombified Lollipop Lady, short, round and wearing a hi-vis jacket, wielding a large stop sign in front of her. She was joined by a Checkout Girl, still in her Moodley Mini-Mart uniform, with a side ponytail, and braces gripped to her now bloodied teeth. They both lurched towards the commotion coming from the north end of town.

Vince and the rest ran terrified from the bus down the street, but had no choice but to stop outside Snipper's salon. Their path ahead blocked by the Checkout Girl and the Lollipop Lady, who growled at them as they advanced unsteadily.

Following from the car park, Snipper and the Goth Witch were closing in fast.

That was not all, though. From the gaps between the buildings, more appeared... among them, a zombified chavvy girl in a Kappa tracksuit and a Dentist. One who was still wearing her surgical mask and brandishing a disturbingly antique drill.

"We're dogmeat." Mikey squeaked.

Suddenly, the Checkout Girl doubled over with a hacking cough, black ooze splattering out of her mouth, and down onto the pavement in revolting fizzy lumps.

Mikey paled as he realized something... he recognized her.

"*Julie*?" he said.

Matt gave Mikey a confused glance. "Wait... You know her?"

"We had a thing once," he said meekly. "It didn't end well at all."

Graham was revolted as Julie expelled another wave of oily bile. "You kissed that? I think I'm going to be sick."

"How do you think I feel?" Mikey shuddered.

Gavin glared at them. "Shut up!" he hissed under his breath. "Don't provoke them."

Too late. Julie had heard and now sprang forward with unexpected speed, tackling Mikey violently onto the street.

. . .

Back on the billboard platform, Patrick moaned in pain, fumbling to wrap his belt around his wounded leg, as blood soaked through the fabric of his jeans.

As the blood slowed, and with shaking and weakening fingers, he opened the duffel bag, desperate to reach the phones and call for help—

His heart sank like a stone, as he realized he had grabbed the wrong bag.

Golf balls.

Hundreds of golf balls stared back at him.

"Fuck my life," he said, deflated.

As he dwelled, he tried to ignore the slow *thud, thud, thud*, coming from below him. Not to mention the tremors that trembled through the billboard with each hit. Ten feet below him, the Bride was hacking determinedly at the billboard's supports, wood splintering under each brutal swing. *Thud, thud, thud.*

In the village below, chaos was in full effect.

Gavin dodged a lethal slash from the Goth Witch's sword as Matt shoved the Chavvie girl back, sending her tripping over a loose brick.

Vince pulled Julie off Mikey, grabbing her by the hair.

At the same time the Lollipop Lady's stop sign came smacking painfully against the back of his head.

"Ow!"

The Lollipop Lady struck again, and again. Harder with each hit.

Vince turned to her, swung Julie around by her hair, and threw her into the Lollipop Lady's path, buying himself a few precious seconds to help Mikey to his feet.

Behind, the Snipper crept in closer, scissors poised inches from Vince's ear. The blades opened, ready to cut when—

A golf ball zipped through the air, smashing hard into her shoulder, spinning her around, as she angrily tried to see what had hit her.

Another ball came flying down, smacking into her head, dropping her to the ground.

Vince stared unbelievingly up at the billboard, where Patrick stood triumphantly, balanced precariously on his one good leg, swinging a broken piece of wooden railing like a baseball bat.

Another golf ball sailed by, missing the Dentist, who was now locked in a bizarre, ineffectual slap-fight with Matt. In the melee of slaps, his finger caught on her surgical mask, ripping it away. Revealing a set of grotesque oversized buck teeth that left him momentarily stunned into inactivity.

Before he could react, another golf ball went whizzing by, narrowly missing Matt's head.

A second then came flying down the road, heading straight for Matt's head. At the last second, he saw it in time and ducked out of its path. The ball rocketed past, missing by millimetres, and collided with the Dentist's mouth, smashing out her teeth in a spray of enamel fragments.

The balls kept coming. Some hit the buildings,

smashing windows, some bounced off down the street, but those that hit, hit hard. Then...

Clang!

A golf ball ricocheted off the Lollipop Lady's stop sign and bounced into the Goth Witch's face, which sent her into a blazing fury. She lunged furiously at Lollipop Lady, swinging her sword high. It met with the stop sign, starting off a battle. Julie soon joined the melee, furious and uncoordinated, all against the Lollipop Lady. None of the zombies were mentally able to process what was happening to them, so they just fought any fight that presented itself. The Dentist didn't join in, though. She simply spat blood, disorientated as she walked about in a daze.

The men stared, bewildered yet oddly entertained as their undead assailants tore into each other with blind rage.

"Shall we start placing bets?" Mikey smiled.

With one decisive swing, the Witch's sword sliced cleanly through the Dentist's neck, sending her head tumbling to the ground.

Gavin nodded appreciatively. "My money's on that one."

Vince looked around, noticing the street southward was clear once more. "Come on, let's go. Everybody stay together."

As they fled down the street, the Snipper's scissors twitched back to life, snipping hungrily at the air. Slowly, her body shuddered awake, snarling as she clambered to her feet, locking her hateful gaze onto the escaping men.

. . .

Everybody stay together. A simple request, but not one these lads followed.

They tore down Moodley's south end like a pack of uncoordinated rats, as they accidentally split off in opposite directions.

Mikey, Graham, and Gavin veered towards Fashion Victemmes, its neon pink signage flickering with sequins. The door was open, and they tumbled inside, bolting it shut behind them.

Vince and Matt broke the other way, heading straight for an old toy shop. Matt hurled himself at the door first, thinking it would be open. But the security chain said otherwise. His face hit the wood hard, as the door didn't budge.

He whimpered in pain as he slowly slid downward.

Vince didn't hesitate as he stepped over Matt, and with one well-aimed boot, the chain broke with a clatter.

Matt got to his feet as Vince pulled him inside.

The toy shop, like the other shops in Moodley, had that dusty, forgotten vibe. The shelves were high, and had been crammed with everything from action figures to porcelain dolls, tin robots to Pokémon plushies. It was a cavern of new and second-hand toys. Displayed with no order at all.

Rubbing his sore nose, Matt blinked through the pain at the shop around them. "Well, this place is bloody creepy," he muttered, eyeing the porcelain dolls, whose glassy stares seemed to follow them around.

Vince didn't say a thing. He had locked the door and was already moving further into the shop. Matt ran alongside him, not wanting to be left alone.

Then, something thumped in the shop.

Somewhere behind a mountain of teddy bears.

Then the bears moved.

Before either could react, a very spotty schoolgirl sprang out from behind the pile. Her uniform was wrinkled and bloody, and she held a large knife in her grip.

She lunged.

Vince barely had time to raise his arms before she rammed the blade straight into his chest.

A grunt escaped him.

He stared down at the blade, and then at her face.

Surprise.

Terror.

Confusion?

He felt no pain.

She stared at him, tilting her head, sizing up her prey, before yanking the knife free.

The plastic blade retracted out of the handle.

It was spring-loaded. It was a toy.

She stabbed again. And again.

Vince just stood there, feeling more insulted than injured.

He balled his fist and punched her straight in the face.

Pop!

A cluster of inflamed zits exploded, causing pus to spray out across his face.

"Christ!" he shouted in disgust.

Matt gagged, turning away with his hand to his mouth.

She reeled, as Vince was shaken, thinking he had just been killed, as he dripped with pus.

"Grab her!" Matt shouted as he raced to the door and flipped the latch.

She was still there, swaying, as her nose bled out black liquid. She still had the toy knife in her hand, and continued ineffectively stabbing Vince with it.

He sneered at her.

The toy shop door opened, and with one hand on either side of her, Matt and Vince threw the spotty girl out into the street.

She landed on the road as they slammed the door shut.

For a second, she just lay there motionless. Until finally, she got to her feet and looked confused.

Inside, Matt and Vince waited by the counter. Hoping nothing more would happen.

Then: *thud*. A soft bump against the door.

They could see her shadow through the frosted door glass.

Matt expected her to smash it in and come after them again.

But another *thud* didn't come.

Through the glass, they saw her silhouette wavering, before she turned and tottered off, swinging the plastic knife out in front of her.

Inside Fashion Victemmes, Gavin and Graham were making themselves useful by checking windows and securing doors.

Mikey, meanwhile, had crept towards the back of the shop. He was busily grumbling to himself. "Should have gone to Marbella, but *noooooo* Mikey, you had to make everyone come to bloody Moodley."

As he walked past a rack of summer dresses, his trainer slipped on something wet. He quickly caught himself, one hand gripping the rail, steadying his balance.

He looked down, and for some reason, even after everything he had witnessed today, he expected to see a puddle of water at his feet.

But it wasn't water, it was blood. A lot of it.

His eyes widened, and he instinctively moved back, only to blindly plant his foot straight into another red patch.

His balance gave way as his foot slid sideways, sending him reeling back into what he immediately assumed was a mannequin.

Today wasn't his day, and it wasn't a mannequin.

It was the source of the blood. A headless corpse that had been hung on a clothes hook.

Mikey yelped as he pushed himself away, back into

the same slick he had just avoided. His foot slipped again, and he collapsed to his knees...

...Right in front of the missing head, which had been perched delicately on a stool, nestled between the rack and a display of half-price feather boas.

Neil came running around the corner, having circled back to town.

His lungs were screaming at him as he wheezed to catch his breath. He had run far too fast and far too far.

Peering over his shoulder, he started to slow down his pace as he realized that Bad Candy was no longer hot on his heels.

He bent double, catching his breath, keeping his eyes around him.

This respite didn't last.

From a doorway came the unmistakable clatter of someone wearing heeled boots. A figure soon emerged out of the shadows, eyes gleaming white. She wore jodhpurs and a tailored green hacking jacket, topped with a velvet riding cap. In her sixties, her white hair was neatly pinned into a bun, and she looked every inch the picture of a middle-class fox hunter, aside for the blood. She was drenched in it from head to toe. Around her neck, she wore a trophy, the gutted remains of a fox, and in her black, gloved grip, she held a riding crop.

As she noticed Neil, she smiled. Not with her mouth as much as with her large, yellowing teeth.

Neil didn't see her until she was right behind him, and had brought the riding crop down across his arse.

He screamed, the sound of a proper, pained yelp. It knocked him forward, and as it did, he fell to the ground.

The Foxhunter was relentless as she advanced, whipping him again and again as he tried to crawl away, but his arse was getting a battering.

Desperate, he looked around, and seeing a couple of stray golf balls on the road, he grabbed one, turned onto his back, and hurled it with all the strength he could muster.

It spun through the air and missed her by over a foot, despite her being only about three feet away from him.

"Oh fuck off," he moaned in annoyance.

Grabbing the second one, he tried again. This time he sat up straight as he threw it.

This one hit.

The ball slammed into her eye socket with a wet squelch, bursting the eyeball, effectively replacing it. The ball stuck out, dimpled, and looked like the eye of a strange giant fly. She stood stunned, blinking her one eye rapidly in confusion.

Neil didn't hesitate.

He was quick to his feet as he spotted an open door in one of the buildings, but as he ran there, something was coming out.

A snarling Granny hobbled from the doorway. She was hunched over a Zimmer frame, dribbling down her chin and growling loudly.

Neil made a quick decision. He needed safety. He could not stay out here in the open.

As if a gift from fate, he saw it. The blood-stained football, sitting on the grass verge.

Without a second thought, he smiled.

Charging forward, he lined up his shot and penalty-kicked the ball.

Zimmer Granny went down like an elderly sack of potatoes as the ball slammed into her face. Neil didn't stop. He vaulted over her and ran into the house, slamming the door and locking it behind him.

Inside, he leaned against the wall, gasping for breath, his backside a battlefield of welts and bruises that stung. He wasn't thinking of the injuries, just of the mocking he would get from everyone if they found out about it.

At the windows on either side of the door, the glass was already starting to fog up with breath and drool, as the Foxhunter and Zimmer Granny looked in hungrily, their faces pressed up like kids outside a sweet shop.

As Neil backed away, he saw them. He could not help but smile. He blew them each a mocking kiss, and for good measure, gave them a double salute—both middle fingers up. One for each of them.

He waggled the left towards the Foxhunter. "This one is for you," he said with a sing-song lilt.

He then waggled his right. "And this one is for you... You creepy old slags."

They did not react. Not a growl nor did they try to break the glass. They just stared in, mainly because they were not looking at him at all.

Clang!

A saucepan smacked Neil over the back of the head, and everything went black.

The Lollipop Lady's stop sign slammed against the barred window of the toy shop. She growled loudly as her attack did nothing.

Inside, Vince was moving between the shelves, looking at every item he could. "Grab anything you can use as a weapon," he said in a hushed voice.

He scanned shelf after shelf. Toy car. Model train. Nothing useful at all... Then he saw the shelf of toy weapons. He rushed over and pawed through the rack, but he found nothing but disappointment. There were foam Klingon bat'leths, rubber nunchucks, plastic swords that lit up in rainbow colours. Useless. Every last bit of it.

He picked up a lightsaber and waved it in the air. It was made of such thin plastic, it would probably break from the air resistance, let alone if he smacked anyone across the face.

He turned, looking for Matt, hoping he had been luckier.

No such luck.

Matt was standing in front of him, clutching a precarious stack of vintage toys in his arms, beaming an idiotically happy grin.

"They're still in their original packaging!" he said, hardly able to contain his joy.

"*Weapons*, Matt, for fuck's sake!" Vince sighed. "Grab any *weapons* you can! You think you can twat one of these bastards over the head with a bloody Ewok?"

The words had barely landed when the shop door handle started to squeak. No rattle. No bang. Just... a squeak, as the handle started to turn.

Matt's joyful smile vanished as he heard it.

"Did you lock the door?" Vince asked.

Matt didn't answer. He was already starting to back up, clutching his toys closer.

Vince didn't bother asking again; he ran over and threw himself against the door, slamming his full weight into it as it started to creak open. The frame slammed shut, not before an arm reached through.

Thin, white, with mottled skin, and a long pair of scissors.

It was the Snipper.

She waved the scissors blindly, hoping to catch any flesh.

Vince screamed as he gripped the plastic lightsaber, and battered the Snipper's trapped limb with as much power as if he were beating her with a blade of grass.

The blades in her hand kept lashing out furiously, slicing through the air only inches from his face.

Matt panicked, looking around for anything that could help.

His eyes caught the remote-control cars behind the till, along with something the shop could only sell to adults: Nitro Fluid.

"Yes!" he exclaimed through gritted teeth as he ran

around the counter and grabbed a bottle from the shelf, as Vince was trying his best to not get skewered by the scissors snipping at him.

Hurrying back over, Matt tore the bottle top off with his teeth.

"Lighter!" he shouted, squirting the Snipper's arm with the fuel.

Vince, now understanding what was happening, dug into his pocket and pulled out his Zippo. But his sweaty fingers fumbled as he tried to open it, and it fell. Hitting the linoleum and skittering under a nearby shelf.

"Fuck!" he shouted.

Matt was already on the case, and dove to retrieve it.

Behind him, the Snipper's scissors jabbed through the gap again, angrier this time, as the smell of the nitro fuel over her now started to sting Vince's eyes.

Matt stood, lighter in hand.

He clicked the lid and sparked it up. Without any hesitation, he tossed the lighter at her arm.

Vince ducked away as the flame ignited instantly. Fire quickly tore up her arm in a sheet of pale blue light, burning the fuel brightly.

Vince let the door open as the flames started to spread, and kicked the Snipper backward. She staggered, retreating into the street, as black smoke curled around her arm, and she was soon engulfed.

Across the street in Fashion Victemmes, Graham peeked

through the heavy curtains that separated the window display from the rest of the shop.

He watched as the Snipper, having been set on fire, thrashed on the floor, dousing the last of the flames. As they were snuffed out, so were her shrieks, which transformed into low growls. She then slowly clambered to her feet and staggered around with the other zombies as if nothing had happened. From behind her, the Foxhunter was clumsily striding up the street to join them, her boots clacking loudly against the road.

"Shit, there's more of them," Graham sighed.

"Get back from the window!" Gavin ordered in a hushed voice. "If they can't see us, they'll forget we're in here."

"That's a bit optimistic, isn't it?" Graham replied, glancing back.

"No. They're easily distracted and confused."

Mikey wasn't part of this conversation. Still at the back of the shop, he'd stepped away from the decapitated body and the severed head. Its milky eyes stared directly at him as he walked away. At least, Mikey thought it looked like that.

He backed up slowly, but as he did, he bumped into something solid that clattered as he hit, causing too loud a noise.

He winced. Dreading what it was, or what that noise might bring.

He looked to his left and saw a blank, plastic face, harmlessly looking at him.

He smiled, relieved... It was just a mannequin.

But to his left, it was not blank.

Not plastic.

And most definitely not harmless.

She stood too still, dressed like she'd raided the clearance rack. Half a dozen price tags clung to her clothes, fluttering like tiny bunting. Her mouth dripped with tar-thick, fizzing, sludge. She stared at Mikey and made a low growl. One that was almost like a purr.

A single gunshot rang out from within the village of Moodley.

It echoed around every shopfront. Every alley. Every open space.

The horde all over town stopped whatever they were doing and paid attention.

Even the sounds of their moaning cut off mid-gargle, as they listened.

High on the billboard, Patrick also heard, looking down the street, half worried someone was hurt, half excited that someone could have weapons that might save them.

With a golf ball still in hand, he had been in mid-attack, hurling them non-stop at the Bride, who remained below. She, too, had paused from hacking at the support columns, alerted by the shot.

Gavin held a smoking pistol.

The woman dressed in Fashion Victemmes' finest, who was about to attack Mikey, had now lost the back of her head. The inside of her skull had painted the shop wall in black goo, brain and gristle. Her body tottered, then dropped like a wet rag.

Mikey turned to the soldier, suddenly livid. "*Now* you decide it's a good time to shoot someone? You fucking wank biscuit!"

"You had a gun all along?" Graham added, aghast.

Gavin didn't answer. He just pointed the pistol at Mikey and instantly pulled the trigger.

Click.

Mikey flinched so hard it looked like he might throw up or soil his pants, or both.

Gavin holstered the now-empty weapon with a shrug. "I was saving the last bullet for when I *really* needed it."

"What?" Mikey muttered, half-flattered.

"Yeah, you're welcome," Gavin added.

"Oh.... I'm... I'm sorry for calling you a wank biscuit," Mikey said sheepishly, before adding. "You're still a twat, though."

Graham, back at the window, said as he peered out again, "I think you just sent out a party invite."

Through the glass, the horde was approaching, walking unsteadily as a group, slouching in their direction.

At the rear of this terrifying pack, trying to keep up at a pace that could only be described as defiant, the

Zimmer Granny slowly shuffled forward. Her walker clunked with every slow step.

Inside the toy shop, with its door now closed and locked, Vince was watching the horde approach Fashion Victemmes.

Matt, meanwhile, with a look of concentrated excitement on his face, was busily fiddling with a large radio-controlled truck. Behind him stood a stack of full nitro fuel cans.

Vince walked over. "They're all going to whatever that bang was," he said, eyeing up the cans. "They *really* sell petrol in toy shops?"

"Nitro fluid," Matt corrected. "It's for radio-controlled cars. Don't you know anything?"

Vince stared at him, then at the toy truck, then at the bottles of explosive fuel stacked beside it.

"I know we need to tool up with something that wasn't made in Taiwan," he said, finally dropping the lightsaber to the floor, which he still had a grip of for some reason.

Moving over to the store's side window, facing the north side of town, Vince could see Patrick resuming his golf ball assault on the chopping Bride below.

He turned to Matt. "So, Mikey, Graham, and the lad from the army are over the road in the clothes shop. Pat's up there." He then looked worried. "What happened to Neil?"

Finger Food

Neil woke with a grunt. He felt the pain in his head before his eyes even managed to open. He knew he was sitting upright. That was the first problem, as he had no recollection of sitting down. The second problem was that he could not move. His hand and feet had both been bound with rope. And the rope was tight. So tight that his body felt numb. He had been strapped to a rickety wooden chair, hands bound to the armrests, ankles lashed to the legs.

As his eyes opened wearily, the lightbulb above made him squint, its brightness intensifying the pain in his head.

He could tell that he was in a kitchen, but this one had been decorated. Streamers and bunting hung across the ceiling, as pink helium-filled balloons floated together in the corner of the room, bumping into each other. One large banner above the window said: *HAPPY 40TH BIRTHDAY.*

His vision was clearing, and he saw the table in front of him. On top was a cake. More specifically, a fondant-icing-covered birthday cake crowned with forty haphazardly burning candles.

Also: fingers.

Human fingers.

Stuck up alongside the candles.

And at the table sat the birthday girl.

If Neil squinted hard and ignored the oozing sores and necrotic flab bursting from the seams of her satin negligee, he might have guessed that her nickname could have been Bubbles, before she'd turned into this demented thing now looking at him. With wild hair like candy floss, eyes sunken like two bruised eggs. She smiled and licked her lips in a kind of flirtatious way that could end in therapy.

Next to the cake, laid delicately on the table, was an electric carving knife. One of her swollen hands stroked it lovingly, as the other reached forward to her cake.

Gingerly, she picked up one of the severed fingers. A thick, hairy finger, the stump of which was coated in a lump of icing.

Without taking her eyes off Neil, Bubbles then lifted the finger to her mouth and suggestively licked the icing off its end. A suggestion he was not liking at all.

Then she did it again. Licking with her blackened, calloused tongue, this time hungrier and more passionate.

Her performance didn't last, though, as she snorted

and bit into the finger like it was pork crackling. The bone crunched between her teeth.

Neil dry-heaved so hard it knocked the chair back an inch. He looked at his own fingers. All there. Still attached. He let out a shuddering, relieved moan.

He then saw the man sat next to him.

Tied to an identical chair a few feet to his left, a man was slumped and very, very lifeless. A party hat had been placed on his lolling head.

The man's hands were a pulp of bloody stumps. Every finger and thumb had been cut off.

Neil didn't recognise him, but he was in life Reginald Pawson. The local councillor. Once plastered on half the lampposts in Moodley. Now plastered to a chair, minus a full set of digits and a pulse.

Neil looked back to Bubbles, sickened. Knowing that this was, in all likelihood, a view into his future. He summoned the last dregs of bravery he could scrape together. It wasn't much, but it was all he had, and all he could think to do.

"This is all very nice, babe," he said, trying for sexy charm and barely managing a nervy quiver, "but how about we forget all that finger food and take this upstairs where it should be? What d'you say?"

Bubbles stopped chewing and stared back at him. Mouth open, and still full of bits of finger.

Neil continued as best he could. "You and I... See, we're both adults, aren't we? I mean, I'm a man... and you... You... You're a..." He couldn't help but gag as he spoke. "You're a woman." He smiled the best smile he had available, which was a weak almost tearful one. "This could be the start of something special between us... All you've got to do is untie me."

Bubbles was doe-eyed and dribbling. She licked her lips as she started to chuckle. Then, she started to slowly slip off her seat, and move under the table. Keeping her eyes on him before she disappeared from view.

Neil gasped. "What are you doing?"

She didn't answer with anything but another chuckle, as her hand reappeared, groped blindly across the table, and found the electric carving knife. She pulled it under with her.

His nervousness spiked. "Oi, what are you doing, babe. Come on, you know we can make this beautiful... No need for power tools now, is there?"

There was movement under the table. A shuffling.

Neil could not move to see where she was.

Then a pop of greasy curls and undead glee, as her face, grinning like a Cheshire Cat with syphilis, reappeared between his knees.

Neil's chair lurched backward, trying to escape, but the legs quickly thudded into the wall. There was no escape.

She clambered on him, her fingers gripping his wrist. She moved fast, not just for someone that size, but for someone that dead. She was somehow faster than the others he had seen.

The electric carving knife screamed to life with a mechanical whirring. The blade buzzed, still with chunks of Reginald's flesh between its teeth, and moved closer.

"Babe," he shouted.

But she was not listening. She was laughing raucously as the blade hovered above one of his little fingers.

Then it bit down.

Through skin, flesh and bone, the carving knife found the wood in a matter of seconds.

Neil howled in agony.

She laughed more, but within her laughter was a pleasurable moan.

Somewhere outside, far away from the domestic nightmare Neil was enduring, a radio-controlled truck zipped down the empty street. A walkie-talkie duct-taped to its flatbed.

It swerved once, then corrected itself. It was as threatening as any toy car would be, but the horde saw it, and disorientated by the noise and sudden movement, twisted around, trying to fight it. But it moved far too fast for them to capture or kill it. Turning in circles, it confused them.

The truck skidded once, reversed, accelerated, and did one tighter circle around them. Making the whole flock bump into each other as they all tried to capture it.

It whipped between their legs and back around for another pass.

Back in the toy shop, Vince and Matt were locked in a battle not unlike two toddlers fighting over the last chocolate. Only this fight involved a remote control and the safety of everyone still breathing.

"Who taught you how to drive?" Matt shouted, reaching for the control. "Let me do it."

Vince shrugged him away. "Ah piss off, ya bell end!"

"Reverse, then. *Reverse!*"

"I know!"

Outside, the truck jerked as it skidded, clipping the Goth Witch straight in the shin, making it almost flip over.

"Bollocks!" Vince shouted.

"Look out! Go back, go back!"

"Shut up, you fucking back seat driver!"

But Matt wasn't wrong. In all fairness, he probably would have done a better job, but Vince did not want to chance that.

At Fashion Victemmes, the radio-controlled truck rammed the front door with a bounce, backed up, and rammed again.

Inside, Mikey, Gavin, and Graham watched it through the window with a wary caution.

The truck rammed again, then again.

"Is someone going to get that?" Gavin asked dryly.

Mikey moved over to the door, slowly, not wanting to draw the attention of any of the women outside.

"Wait," Graham said, leaning closer to the window. "A couple of them are still looking this way... Wait... Wait... *Go!*"

Mikey flung the door open, and the truck zipped in. As it moved, the women noticed Mikey and advanced.

The Goth Witch's face hit the door as it slammed shut. Her mouth smeared her unpleasant, black oil across the glass, as her lips pressed against it like a leech.

"Jesus," Mikey said, backing away from the door's eyeline, away from the undead eyes locked onto him.

Vince's voice crackled from the radio duct-taped to the pickup.

'Hello? Are we in?'

Graham peeled the tape off and picked up the toy walkie-talkie. He noticed that on the back was the logo for the *A-Team*, and he could not help but smile as he clicked on the talk button.

"I take it you're in the toy shop?"

'Who's over there?' Vince replied. *'Is Neil with you?'*

Graham shook his head. "Nah mate. It's just me, Mikey, and the Milky Bar Kid."

"My name's Gavin," the soldier grunted.

"Whatever." Graham said. "Anyway, the speed Neil was running, he's probably home by now."

But Neil wasn't home.

He was strapped to a chair, teeth clenched, watching his own severed pinkie get dunked delicately into the birthday cake icing, like it was a biscuit in tea.

Bubbles licked the cream off with a satisfied moan. Her whole body heaved with pleasure as she tasted his flesh.

. . .

In Fashion Victemmes, Mikey had picked up the remote-controlled truck and was looking over it with a child-like fascination.

Graham, still on the radio, sighed. "So, what's the plan, Vince?"

A pause.

Vince's reply was agitated. *'What do you mean what's the plan?'*

Graham looked confused. "The plan. What's the plan?"

'I haven't got a plan. Why the fuck is it up to me? What's your plan?'

"I've got a plan," Mikey offered helpfully.

Graham ignored him. "What's all this bollocks with these radios then, if you don't have any plan? Kinda lends itself to that conclusion, don't you think?"

Back in the toy shop, Vince slumped against the shelf, talking into the walkie-talkie.

"I just fancied a chat with someone about something other than fucking Star Wars."

'Oh, right. How is Matt?' Graham asked.

Matt was currently not hearing any of the conversation and was busily taping the Zippo lighter to the barrel of a Super Soaker.

Vince stared over at him, deadpan. "The force is with

him, apparently," he said. "Building weapons like McGuyver."

Not far away, Bubbles was preparing to add another candle to her cake, but first she needed to finish her mouthful.

"Oi!" Mikey shouted.

Gavin and Graham looked up from the conversation with Vince, synchronised in their mutual exasperation.

"What?" they both barked.

"I *said* I've got a plan."

Five minutes later, all three men in the dress shop were looking down at the severed head from the back of the store.

It sat slumped on the stool, eyes bulging with posthumous alarm, jaw half open in a look of surprise. Even he couldn't believe how this evening was going.

"Go on then," Gavin urged.

"Me?" Mikey replied, backing off. "You're supposed to be the double hard bastard. You do it."

"It's your plan, arsehole."

"You two are so gay," Graham said, stepping between them. "You two should fuck and be done with it." He crouched, grabbed the head by what little hair was left on its pate, like it was nothing but a melon, and carried it over to the radio-controlled truck, now on the glass-topped counter.

No ceremony. Just disgust. Just getting it done.

He wedged the head onto the flatbed, then secured it with several rounds of tape from the nearby dispenser. Along the tape, the words *Special Offer* was repeatedly printed.

Mikey picked up the walkie-talkie.

"The payload has been delivered, I repeat, the payload has been delivered."

'What the fuck are you talkin' about, lad?' Vince crackled back, his voice distorted through the cheap speaker.

"The severed head is in the toy truck you sent over," Mikey reiterated clearer. "Are you ready?"

Vince was crouched by the window, staring out like a soldier pinned down by enemy fire, radio in his hand.

"Yeah, ready," he said. "Listen, don't mess around out there, Mikey. I know you've nicked your fair share of motors, but this isn't the old bill you're dealing with this time. You screw this up and you're looking at something worse than a slapped wrist and a bit of community service, you get me?"

There was a pause.

"No wonder his old lady left," Mikey sighed before

clicking on the talk button again. "Yeah, whatever, Vince. Ten-four. Roger that. Here comes dinner."

Clipping the walkie-talkie to his belt, Mikie joined Graham by the door.

Outside, the horde was still gathered like rabid shoppers at the January sales, clawing mindlessly at the window.

"You know," Graham said in thought. "We're gonna need a diversion for our diversion." He and Mikey looked at Gavin, who was peering through the curtains behind the window display.

Gavin soon saw their look, and sighed.

"Fine," he grumbled. Before gritting his teeth and pushing himself forward through the curtain, into the display. In full view of the waiting undead.

Arms raised. Feet stomping. Jazz hands out and his body in full gyration. The performance he put on was pure, unrehearsed panic, but his intended audience didn't care about technique.

They turned towards him instantly.

A dozen swollen and veiny faces lit with rage. The whole cluster surged towards the window, snarling as they staggered forward.

"Good," Graham smiled, as he peered at the dispersing women from the front door. "Ready?" he added to Mikey.

Mikey was. He held the remote-controlled truck, complete with taped-on head, and held it in front of him like it was somehow dangerous.

As Graham opened the door, Mikey squeezed his

eyes shut and ran out, dropped the truck on the pavement, then hurried back in. Not one of the women had a clue he had come out, they were still enchanted by the horribly unsexy performance Gavin was putting on.

Vince saw the truck get placed outside Fashion Victemmes, and straight away twisted the transmitter controls.

"Come and get your Meals on Wheels," he mumbled as the truck sputtered into motion, its motor whining loudly under the added weight of the head upon it.

The horde all turned to see what the noise was, and began to follow, stumbling, twitching, trailing viscous fluid behind them like they were slug tracks. They followed the small truck down the street, south towards the church, drawn like moths. They growled and lunged as the head rolled away, out of reach.

The plan was very much working.

Mikey then took his chance.

He ran back out through the shop door and bolted north.

On the billboard platform, Patrick sat cross-legged, earphones in, swaying as the Bride still hacked at the wooden supports below.

He pulled the headphones out and sat up straight, as he saw Mikey darting up the street towards him. Something was happening and he had zero idea what.

. . .

Mikey reached the Range Rover at the edge of the car park. It sat under the orange glow of the streetlamp, smeared with dirt and blood, but still intact. He grabbed the door handle.

Locked.

Of course it was.

He spotted a loose rock by the kerb, and rushed over to pick it up.

Vince was peering out of the window, controller still in hand, eyes locked through the glass, down the street. The truck was still moving, but in fits and starts, and not in a straight line. Matt was now behind him, annoyingly watching and offering commentary.

"This thing's handling like a supermarket trolley," Vince moaned.

"It's the extra weight," Matt said, peering out. "You should turn it around or it's going to go out of range."

Vince carried on doing what he was doing.

"Turn it!" Matt insisted. "You gotta turn it!!"

The truck juddered around the south end of the street, skidding past the church steps. The hoard followed, bumping and scraping into each other, too focused to give up, too slow to catch up.

But then, the truck clipped the kerb, forcing it to roll up onto two wheels.

Vince and Matt leaned the opposite way to the truck instinctively, as if the weight of their bodies could alter the remote-controlled vehicle's trajectory.

The truck dropped back down to the ground with a clattering thump. It bounced once, then hit a patch of debris, launching it cleanly into the air.

It soon landed on all fours like a pro, back on track.

In the toy shop, the two of them burst into fits of laughter. For a second, just a second, it was hilarious. They were little boys again.

Up at the Range Rover, Mikey lobbed the rock at the driver's window. He was *determined*. He was going to *do this*. He was *the man*. He was also not very good at throwing.

It bounced off the frame of the car's door, and ricocheted back at him, directly into his chest.

He dropped, clutching his ribs and gasping in pain.

. . .

Under the billboard, the Bride paused, hearing the agonized yelp.

She turned slowly, sniffing the air. Her eyes widened hungrily as she saw Mikey on the ground next to the Range Rover.

With an exhalation of black fluid and a moan of pleasure, she forgot the billboard, and started to shamble over to where her new prey was.

Patrick didn't hesitate.

"Oi! Up here!" he shouted, and threw a golf ball with surprisingly perfect aim.

It clipped her skull with a crack.

She paused.

There was no pain, but the hit grabbed her attention. She turned and looked up, eyes filled with hungry hellfire.

"Yeah, that's right," Patrick called out, swinging his legs over the side to her. "That dress makes your arse look fat."

She snarled. Took a few steps back. Then charged towards the billboard.

She did not even drop the axe from her hand as she rammed her body into the half-hacked wooden support.

The whole thing shook violently as she collided.

His plan had horribly backfired.

Patrick was thrown off the platform, only just managing to catch himself on the edge by his fingertips, dangling off the side of the billboard above her.

"No, no, no, no, no," he begged, as he tried to pull himself back up to safety.

. . .

Mikey regained just enough wind to stand. He picked up the same rock again, squared his stance, and hoped to every God imaginable that this would work.

He sprinted towards the window with everything he had.

He brought the rock around, throwing it with all his might.

The stone careened from his hand, and the moment played out in his eyes in almost slow motion. This, of course, made it doubly annoying, as the same thing happened again. The rock bounced off the glass, and it came flying back his way, thankfully missing him by an inch and landing on a nearby verge.

Further down the street, the remote-controlled truck was still bouncing along, but the horde had almost got it surrounded.

It weaved through puddles, kicked up splashes of dirt, and zigzagged between their legs.

Then it accidentally collided with the Snipper's foot, where it stopped dead in its tracks.

The Snipper looked down, in a gargling fury.

"Oh shit," Matt exclaimed, seeing the truck predicament.

Vince's expression turned to panic. He threw the truck into reverse.

. . .

The wheels were whirring in protest. The engine whined, until the remote-controlled truck got some traction and managed to dismount the Snipper's shoe.

It was soon moving back up the street.

But not fast enough. The incline was too great to ascend as fast as it had come down.

The Snipper stalked towards it fast.

"Come on, Mikey!" Graham shouted into the radio.

Gavin was at the window, no longer dancing as he stared out. "Come on!" he pleaded.

Matt stared through the window of the Toy Shop door looking at the truck: "Come on!"

Vince clenched his teeth, pushing the control into reverse as firmly as he could: "Get up there, you slag!"

But the truck was lagging back up the hill. The head on its flatbed bounced, the Special Offer tape starting to come loose.

The horde was closing in fast.

Gavin sighed seeing Mikey's ineffectual rock throwing. "He's fucked it."

For once, Graham didn't disagree.

The truck veered back into the kerb and lost the fight, sending it spinning.

It spun once and then tipped onto its side. Scraping along the street. Its wheels spun uselessly in the air for a moment before finally winding down. The toy lay still. The head in the flatbed stared up helplessly.

The Snipper didn't waste any time.

She was on it in seconds, her face contorted into a malevolent glee, as her scissors dropped beside her. She ripped the head from the flatbed, and didn't waste any time before biting into its cheek.

The others were soon next to her to get a taste. All of them piling around, reaching for the head, trying to get their own bite.

Up by the billboard, the Bride bent down to pick up her axe from the grass.

The moment she was distracted, and as the billboard stopped shaking, Patrick took his chance. He hauled himself back up onto the platform with a supreme effort and a loud grunt.

Flopping onto the thin platform, he immediately reached for his bag of ammunition. By the fistful, he grabbed the golf balls and started hurling them down at her.

He was not the Patrick of five minutes ago. He was now beyond the fear. He was just really pissed off.

"You want a fight?" he screamed, throwing the balls, one after the other. "Here's your fucking fight!"

Mikey was still having his own small disaster.

He held the rock in his hand and—learning a lesson by not attempting to throw it again— hammered it against the Range Rover's window.

But nothing happened. The glass was reinforced and didn't so much as shudder.

In a last burst of frustration, he dropped the rock to the ground and kicked the vehicle's door.

It wasn't even a hard kick, but as his boot touched the chassis, the siren-like alarm started to blare. A wailing, electronic shriek that cut through the quiet around him. The headlights soon joined in, flashing along to the cacophony.

The horde stopped trying to feast on the severed head, and turned to look up the street where the noise was coming from.

Each had managed at least one bite, their jaws now moist with blood and brains freshly scooped from the open skull in the Snipper's hands.

. . .

Mikey kicked the car again, shouting in frustration "What's this thing made of..."

The alarm cut off.

"...fucking *kryptonite*?!"

His voice echoed as the noise stopped.

Shit, he thought, as he turned to look around, fearing the worst.

Down by the shops, illuminated by the streetlights and hazy moonlight, the horde were all silent, staring up at him.

Vince was watching from the toy shop window.

"Mikey, run," he yelled into the walkie-talkie. "They've spotted you."

Vince's voice rang out from the radio strapped to Mikey's belt.

He didn't argue.

He raced to find shelter.

First shop: locked.

"Shit!"

Second shop: locked.

"Fuck!"

Third shop: the door opened.

He practically fell inside, kicking the door shut with enough force to rattle the nearby window.

He stopped, catching his breath.

The sign in the window flickered a single word repeatedly. A word he didn't even notice: *MEAT*.

This was a butcher's shop. Even in the low light, he could smell that much.

As he stepped further inside and his eyes adjusted, he noticed rows of pale meat slabs hanging from iron hooks behind the counter, swinging slightly in the breeze he had just caused.

Then another smell hit him. Not the sour scent of raw mince, but something sharper and much fouler.

Mikey figured the meat must be going off. The air wasn't nearly as cold as it should have been in here, and when he laid a hand on the display glass, it was warm to the touch. The refrigeration was off.

He glanced over his shoulder to make sure no one had caught up to him, but thankfully, the street outside was still clear.

He needed to find a back door. Make it round to the back of the toy shop and try and get in there. That was the plan.

He crept around the counter and approached the row of hanging meat.

He squinted at them as he walked by, not liking the idea of being that close to carcasses, farmyard or otherwise.

On the last slab on the row, something made him stop and back up against the tiled wall.

This was not meat from any farmyard.

He saw a tattoo.

Inked across the wide stretch of skin was a Celtic

knot pattern, with the words *Mum & Dad*, tattooed in cursive beneath it.

He started to gag, but had no time to examine any more, because he heard something.

A sound from the back room.

A thumped chopping.

CHOP.

CHOP.

CHOP.

Mikey turned towards the front door. He had a choice. Run back into the jaws of a bunch of bloodthirsty zombies, or through this plastic curtain and into the back room. Through to where this noise was coming from.

CHOP.

CHOP.

CHOP.

How bad could it be? he thought, before looking at the tattooed meat again.

CHOP.

CHOP.

CHOP.

He had no real choice. It was like one of those drunken questions Neil was always so fond of asking when he was five pints in.

'Gun to your head, would you rather sweat mayonnaise or cry baked beans?'

'Gun to your head, you're trapped in a room with a ghost and a chimp on ket. Who do you reason with to get out?'

'Gun to your head, would you rather be hunted every Sunday by a slow-moving pensioner with a knife... or once a year, wake up in Belgium with no pants and a receipt for something called "The Deep Sponge"?'

'Gun to your head, you gotta watch your mum wanking every night, or change your name to Peter File?'

'Gun to your head, would you rather gobble off your grandad or eat out your mum?'

Here, the quandary was run towards many zombies, or... whatever the hell awaited him here.

CHOP.

CHOP.

CHOP.

He moved back a strip of plastic with trembling fingers.

And there she was.

CHOP.

CHOP.

CHOP.

The Butcher. Built like a chest freezer in an apron, and wearing large rubber gloves. In her hand, she held a huge cleaver.

She was covered head to foot in blood. Old and new. Every part of her was literally dripping red.

On the butchers' block in front of her was a body, or at least what remained of one. Limbs. Chunks. Torn meat.

And next to that, and what Mikey could not stop staring at, was a large glass bowl. A bowl filled to the brim with dicks and balls. So many chopped genitals, now in a soggy pile.

She raised the cleaver high, oblivious to Mikey's presence.

Then Vince's voice crackled over the radio on Mikey's belt.

'Mikey, you there, lad? You okay?'

The Butcher stopped.

Mikey winced.

The radio hissed static again, as Vince repeated. *'Mikey?'*

The Butcher's head turned very slowly, the cleaver remaining up.

Her eyes locked on him as her huge, bloody brow furrowed.

Then she roared.

She threw her cleaver at him, missing by a breath, as it embedded in the wall next to his face. He flung himself backward into the shop, knocking off the human remains from the hooks as he went.

Holy Carnage

Vince was already moving towards the toy shop door.

"Come on! Stop pissin' around," he shouted impatiently.

Matt was crouched, hunched over the Super Soaker, still working on it.

"I'm not going out there half-cocked," Matt replied, carefully twisting the last bottle of nitro fluid into place.

Then, with a dramatic flourish only a lifelong geek could manage, he flung the empty container aside, grabbed the super soaker, cocked the pump, and stood up.

"Let's party," he stated with a sneer full of swagger, bred from years of watching cheesy action films.

Vince held his hand held out. "Okay... Where's mine?"

Matt paused, his superhero stance reduced to an apologetic one. "This was the only one like this," he said.

"But you can take this one." He reached into his belt and pulled out a second weapon.

It was a small, plastic pistol, shaped like a Beretta. The sort of thing you got in a cereal box or at a bad market stall.

He threw it over to Vince, who stared in annoyance. "What's this going to do?"

Matt shrugged. "Make you feel sexy?"

Vince squeezed the trigger, and a jet of nitro fluid spurted out with a wheezy hiss. It's spray barely reached a metre away.

Matt raised the Super Soaker again, summoning his bravery once more.

"Let's do it," he said. "You and me. Like Butch and Sundance."

"They both died, you gimp."

Matt's grin didn't falter. "Yeah. But they looked bloody cool doing it."

They burst out of the toy shop, pretty much exactly like Butch and Sundance, complete with half a plan. Vince first, Matt behind, both charging into the street with their makeshift weapons held out, screaming their best battle cries.

The horde had moved on, trailing northward to find Mikey in their mindless shuffle. Only one remained, staring at them... The Goth Witch. She was in the middle of the street, waiting with her large sword in hand, waving it about like a Goth lady Conan. On her face was an expression of pure insanity and bloodthirsty malice.

Her blade sliced through the air towards Matt, a fast swing that would've halved him if Vince hadn't seen her in time. He lunged and pushed Matt sideways, knocking him off balance. The sword missed by inches, thankfully splitting air instead of flesh.

Then Vince shot his tiny plastic pistol.

He squeezed the trigger repeatedly, not letting up, not aiming, just trying to hit any part of her. The nozzle spurted arcs of nitro fluid at her like a squeaky water fountain, drenching her face in its combustible liquid.

She screamed in anger, as a stream of black, oily fluid dribbled out.

Pouncing, her cloak flowed behind her as she moved. She slammed straight into Vince. He staggered but didn't fall. He managed to grab her sword arm and fight back, pretending he knew what he was doing. He wrestled with her cloak, yanked it over her head, and spun her around.

"Do it!" he shouted. "Matt! Do the fire thing. *Now!*"

Matt lit the Zippo where it was duct-taped to the Super Soaker's barrel. The flame ignited, caught, and with one desperate pump, he pulled the trigger.

A jet of fire sprayed out of the nozzle.

The first burst missed Vince by the width of a prayer, but hit the Goth Witch head-on. She caught fire immediately. Her screams rose an octave with every second of burning, her body throwing itself about trying to stop it, but the flames were unforgiving as they started to eat at every part of her.

Blinded, she swung her sword, but had no idea where they were.

Matt and Vince had both backed away instinctively, retreating towards the pub as she fell about in circles, the fire consuming her clothes, hair, and flesh.

Then she ran.

Straight past them, down the street, squealing like a teakettle. With no idea where she was going, she vanished around the corner in a wailing mass of smoke.

Matt lowered the Super Soaker. "I think we did damn well, don't you th—"

The nozzle of the plastic toy hissed, as the end of the gun suddenly caught fire.

"Shit, shit, shit, shit!" he yelped, waving the gun around, trying to put the fire out. But the flames climbed all over its plastic shell.

He dropped the weapon instantly. And as he did, the soaked ground in front of him lit like a fuse. Fire slithered across the nitro fluid back inside the toy shop, where he had absent-mindedly dribbled a trail.

For a heartbeat, it was silent, and Matt and Vince could only stare.

Then the shelves inside the shop ignited.

BOOM.

The explosion punched at them like a fist. A fireball belched out through the toy shop door, sending glass and smoke hurtling out.

They were thrown back and hit the ground face-first.

Soon, the noise died down and the flames just burned away at the rest of the building. Cinders floated down on the street in small glowing specks, like dozens of falling fireflies.

Vince sat up coughing, his coat smouldering, his eyebrows singed.

Something thudded between his legs, metal, scuffed, still warm: The Zippo. It had found its way back to him again.

He picked it up, held it between his fingers for a moment, before the sound of smashing glass made him turn.

Mikey came flying out of the butcher shop window, having been thrown through it. Right at the feet of the waiting horde. And only a few steps behind, the gigantic Butcher climbed out of the smashed window after him, knocking out the rest of the jagged glass away with her cleaver.

He had zero inclination to hang around and become a meal.

He scrambled to his feet, ignoring the pain, and sprinted away, narrowly missing the swing of the Lollipop Lady's stop sign. He pelted down the road like a kid chased by dogs, every limb thrashing about, face full of unfiltered terror.

The rest of the horde were about to pursue, but backed away as the Butcher snarled at them. They all were told that this kill was hers.

. . .

"Fuck, fuck, fuck, fuck, fuck," Mikey shouted in a panic, as he skidded around the corner, the walkie-talkie flying from his belt mid-sprint. He didn't notice, and even if he did, he wouldn't care. He crashed against the door of Fashion Victemmes and pounded his fists upon it.

Graham quickly let him in. Opening just enough for Mikey to fall inside. Just in time too, as the Butcher arrived a heartbeat later.

She slammed her cleaver against the door. The frame shuddered under the force.

She then bellowed in frustration.

Vince and Matt watched from behind a nearby post box.

The Butcher was massive. A blood-soaked goliath, with hands the size of spades.

"Do we try and take her down?" Matt whispered. "Set her on fire?"

"She's a bit of a big girl," Vince replied. "And my gun ain't that big."

Matt didn't argue.

Behind them, the rest of the horde had begun to reappear through the smoke.

"What are we supposed to do?" Matt asked.

Vince looked at the monsters approaching, then to the butcher. "What are we supposed to do? We do what everyone else does when they're facing their own mortality... We cheese it."

They ran. Fast. Away from the slow-approaching crowd and the roaring butcher.

They did not stop until they got to the foot of the church.

Bounding up the steps, across a carpet of old, wind-scattered confetti, they did not look back.

"I bet it's locked," Matt said as he grabbed the large wooden door's handle and pushed it down.

Much to both their surprise, it opened.

"Some good luck for a change!" Matt laughed as he turned to Vince.

Neither of them saw the Vicar lunging at them.

She came from the shadows, all robes and blotchy skin, her eyes bulging with holy murder. She reached out of the doorway and clamped her hands around Matt's throat.

Vince didn't pause.

He leaned in and punched her. Once and very hard on the bridge of the nose.

She fell back through the doorway, crashing onto the stone slab floor among more fallen confetti. A puff of paper hearts and stars flew around her as she landed.

Quickly getting inside, Vince crossed himself. Not that he believed, but just in case. He didn't believe in zombies either. But here they were.

This was not what Vince or Matt had expected to find in the Holy Trinity Catholic Church. One that served the village of Moodley, as well as the surrounding farmland.

The whole of the nave had been gutted. Gone were the pews and hymnals. As well as all traces of the religion that this place had been built for. The Altar was gone, the font, the statues. Nothing remained, aside from the tall stained-glass windows, and a row of confessional booths along one side.

It was a military nerve centre that occupied this once-sacred space. But even that had been destroyed.

After hurling the unconscious body of the Vicar out of the door and locking it behind them, they turned back to the church. Not taking the silence for granted.

The air smelled like burning plastic, and it was hard for either Matt or Vince to breathe. Rows of smashed electronic equipment were around them. Blackened and burned wires curled out of the broken terminals. The monitors that had not been smashed flickered with white static, casting the otherwise dark room in a cold glow.

Vince stopped in the centre of the nave and glanced around, looking at every corner of the damage. It wasn't just the broken machines here, *Vote Meg Nut* posters had been plastered upon most of the stone walls, and were now all blood-spattered and torn.

In the corner, large wooden crates had been stacked, each stencilled in neat military font: *ARMY: BIOHAZARD*.

Matt and Vince were not the only people here. Just the only ones in one piece. There was half a leg here, an arm still holding a radio there. A torso slumped between two chairs. All clothed in torn remnants of their military uniforms. What was left was unrecognisable and incomplete.

"Don't ever let me take the piss out of your

conspiracy theories again." Vince said, without a trace of humour.

Matt was too shocked at the carnage to reply.

They moved cautiously forward across this ruined control centre.

Vince motioned towards the machines. "This is a good time to be a nerd, Matt. Get on those and figure out how to make something work. Something has gotta still do something."

In the middle of the village, something was working. Just not something in Vince or Matt's favour.

The walkie-talkie, the one that had fallen from Mikey's belt, lay abandoned on the street.

'Hey, guys,' it crackled with Vince's voice. *'Me and Matt are in the church. And you won't believe what we're looking at.'*

A pale and clammy hand reached down. Huge and rotting.

Graham, Mikey, and Gavin were slumped on the floor behind the window display curtain. They had barricaded themselves in this shop the best they could.

They sat in silence, waiting, but had no idea what for.

Then, a faint voice drifted from outside, distant but unmistakable. The Scouse accent belonging to Vince.

'Hey, where the bleedin' hell are you lot?'

Graham looked around. "Where's our radio?"

Mikey reached for his belt. But as he felt nothing there, a slow dread crept across his face.

'*Graham? Mikey? Lads?*'

They all turned and peered through a gap in the curtain.

There was the walkie-talkie, in the hands of the Butcher.

'*Anyone there?*' Vince's voice crackled again. '*We're in the church.*'

The Butcher tilted her head, looking down at the small device in wonder. Without any thought beyond hunger and murder, she raised the radio to her mouth and tried to bite a chunk out of it. Plastic cracked under her teeth. She scowled, disappointed, and threw the walkie-talkie back to the ground. Letting out an annoyed grunt, she walked over to the clothing shops, sniffing the air, knowing her prey was still inside.

It wasn't long before she began pacing back and forth in front of the windows, scraping her cleaver along the glass as she moved. Letting out high-pitched squeals.

Behind her, the rest of the horde slowly approached. Unable to see anything beyond the window display, nothing except their own reflections.

A couple of them started to drift away from the murderous mindset, their brains unable to remember why they were there. As if rage and purpose had drained out of them, leaving only the habits they'd clung to in their life. Using the window as a mirror, the Barmaid clutched a lipstick and reapplied it with an unsteady hand. Next to her, the Chavvie Teenager brushed her hair with clawed fingers. A few of the others stood gormlessly looking in at the mannequins, mirroring their vacant stares and poses.

Then the Butcher clunked her cleaver into the glass.

As she did, a crack appeared, splintering outward.

The boys dropped out of sight instantly, closing the curtain.

"That can't be good," Graham said. "We *have* to get out of here."

"And go where?" Mikey asked.

"We follow your mates to the church," Gavin suggested, then immediately checked his watch.

Mikey turned. "Did you not see the size of that meat cleaver?"

But Gavin wasn't listening. He was suddenly focused, curiously so. "We need to get to the church, *now*," he said. "It's our best chance."

"It's a bit late to start praying." Mikey laughed.

Gavin was about to start shouting his reply, when he noticed that Graham was smiling, stifling a laugh.

"You feeling alright, mate?" Gavin asked.

Graham turned, unable to hide his smile. "I've just had a *genius* fucking idea," he said.

Fifteen minutes later...

The dressing room doors in Fashion Victemmes creaked open one by one.

Graham stepped out first, looking like a mannequin that had fallen out of the back of a Debenhams lorry.

The dress was oversized. The heels were too big. His wig was askew. But he wore it with the swagger of a man who'd stopped caring several traumas ago. He felt that he looked fantastic. He was wrong.

Mikey followed and looked somehow worse.

His shirt was too short, his crop top too tight, and he had also chosen a terrible straw hat to wear, underneath which a wig sat like a dead squirrel. Not to mention, he wore the same mucky trainers he had come to Moodley in, giving the whole look a post-apocalyptic hooker vibe.

Gavin stepped out last.

He looked... disturbingly beautiful.

Tights perfect. Hairline sharp. His dress fit perfect. And somehow, he had also found time to apply make-up. There was a faint shimmer to his eyeshadow, that showed the care in his craft.

The others stared at him.

Gavin noticed. "What?"

Graham looked at him suspiciously. "You've done this before, haven't you?"

"Don't you get any funny ideas," Gavin replied.

"Don't worry," Mikey said. "He's not a lesbian... I'm the one you should look out for."

"Come on then guys," Graham grinned. "Show us your walks. This has to be believable."

Mikey, resigned, gave it a go. Something between a toddler learning to run and a giraffe discovering ice.

"Swing your hips a bit more," Graham urged. "Mikey, you *have* to swing your hips." He quickly stepped forward. "Like this," his steps were exaggerated and a bit ludicrous. "Find your inner woman with each step. Okay?" He turned and grabbed Mikey's sides. Moving his hips in a guided, slow, sway.

"Alright. Get your mitts off," Mikey slapped him away. "I can find my inner woman myself, thank you very much!"

Then they turned to Gavin, who looked at them with a raised eyebrow.

He walked without another word.

Effortless. Elegant. The kind of walk that made men turn.

"Is there something you want to tell us, Gary?" Graham asked. "You batting for my team, huh?"

"My bloody name is *Gavin*."

"Except on Saturday night," Mikey added with a smile, "when it's Peaches."

Gavin sighed. "Is this going to work or what?"

A sound came from the front of the shop, as if on cue. That familiar squeal.

The Butcher was back at the glass, dragging her cleaver across it with slow, deliberate menace.

The crack in the window deepened.

Outside the dressing rooms, the three looked at each other.

Graham nodded. "Guess now is as good a time as any."

The Butcher paced the pavement with the lumbering menace.

She went up to the Mini-Mart, turned, then came back again, dragging her cleaver along all the windows, sniffing as she went. When she passed the window display of Fashion Victemmes, something had changed.

Graham was there, absolutely still in the window display, wedged between two mannequins.

The Butcher slowed, finding something not quite right about it.

But the undead weren't experts in subtle distinctions. After a pause, she moved on, dragging her cleaver along the glass in a long, teeth-aching scrape.

Then she turned back again.

This time in the window display, Graham had gone, and in his place stood Mikey.

She stopped once more. Leaned in. Her face close to the window, her breath misted up the glass. She sniffed in heavier. She stared, unblinking.

Mikey held still, every muscle clenched, dressed in his ill-fitting drag and silently praying it would work.

The Butcher couldn't quite figure it out. She smelt the crack in the glass more, but could not figure it out. With a grunting snort, she moved on again.

Mikey rushed back from the window display.

"I could almost smell her breath!" he said, wiping the sweat from his lip.

Graham pointed to Gavin. "You're up, soldier boy."

Gavin adjusted his wig with a confident ease,

stepping into the display. "If she bought you two, I think I'll be just fine."

Graham stared at Mikey, who was now scratching his groin with the vigour of a farm dog. The miniskirt constricting him uncomfortably.

"What?" Mikey said defensively.

Gavin, of course, was right. The Butcher walked by without even stopping.

A few laps of pacing later, a new mannequin had been shoved unceremoniously into the window display. This mannequin had a beard, crudely drawn on with black marker, and it was wearing Gavin's camouflage jacket.

When the Butcher took one look at it, she reacted like a cat seeing a laser dot. She charged the window, and immediately went into a frenzy, rabidly pounding and scraping at the glass.

While she raged, Graham, Mikey, and Gavin slipped out of the shop in their new garb. Looking on a scale from tragic to fabulous. Sauntering away towards the church.

Beneath the village billboard, the Bride stood eerily still. Almost dormant and catatonic. Her eyes were even more vacant than usual, as if whatever had driven her before had now short-circuited.

From above, Patrick stared down, shifting his weight and craning his neck to peer over the edge.

But as he moved, his leg caught the duffel bag,

knocking the last golf ball out onto the platform. It rolled to the edge, and before he could stop it, it dropped down.

"Shit," he mumbled.

It fell straight down onto the Bride's head with a gentle *bonk*.

Her eyes opened.

As Patrick was cursing himself for losing his last ball, the three men in drag sashayed down towards the south end of Moodley.

Well. Two men and Gavin. He was far too good at this to be considered a man. He was effectively channelling a woman at 200%.

They swung their handbags like it was the Queen's parade, each doing their best impression of womanhood under pressure. Inside the bags were their normal clothes, pushing each bag to the brink of bursting.

From the horde, the Snipper watched with a terrifying stare. She didn't attack. Their ruse seemed to be working perfectly.

Gavin had fully committed. Hips swinging, shoulders loose, lips pouted. He was giving the performance of a lifetime and getting away with it.

The horde was fooled.

The Barmaid sloppily reapplied her lipstick once more. The Chavvie Teenager blinked vacantly at her reflection.

But one did not fall for it.

Julie.

She took one look at Mikey and knew something was amiss.

In the middle of the street, Graham paused by the discarded walkie-talkie.

Gavin, in full swagger, not looking where he was going, bumped into the back of him.

"Why are we stopping?" he whispered.

Slowly, trying not to be noticed, Graham bent down, still pouting, still trying to ignore every masculine instinct, yet still coming across as a terrible caricature. He daintily picked up the walkie-talkie, pressed his thumb on the button, and spoke quietly into it the mic.

"Vince? You there?"

No answer.

Across the village, the radio sat on a table in the church. Echoing around the nave.

'Can you get ready?' Graham spoke among the static. *'We're on our way to you.'*

Up on the billboard, Patrick was watching them saunter down the street. Or gawping, more like. Even from this distance, he could tell it was Mikey and Graham. He squinted, laughing, lost in his amused shock, and did not notice that the Bride had begun hacking at the supports once more. And he hadn't realized how much progress she'd made.

The next swing of her axe rang out. The one after that, louder still, now grabbing his attention, as the whole structure started to wobble and groan beneath him.

Patrick knew he had no more time.

One more chop was all it took, and the billboard gave out with a splintering cry. The whole structure lurched forward.

"Oh, shiiiiiiiiiiiit," Patrick cried out as gravity claimed him.

He turned to grab onto anything and only managed to grip the peeling corner of the razor blade ad. It didn't hold, as it tore down under his weight, showing more of the tampon advert below.

The whole thing folded down, crashing across the entrance car park in a cacophony of cracking, bending metal and snapping wood, blocking the only way out of town.

He hit the ground hard, as pain surged from his wounded leg, causing it to bleed even worse. His jeans not holding back the dripping red.

Groaning, he rolled over, dragging himself upright.

He looked around for the Bride, nervously expecting her to launch at him with her axe, but she was nowhere.

Limping to his feet, almost crying out from the agony, he rushed as fast as he could towards the nearby open minibus and climbed inside.

It was not empty.

There was Bad Candy once more, in front of him, twirling one of his golf clubs like it was a baton.

Patrick should have turned and run, but he found his temper snapping once more. His meditative progress failed as he hobbled towards her. "That's my nine iron!" he barked furiously, yanking it from her grip.

Getting back off the minibus, he hit the close button, trapping Bad Candy inside once more.

He had the golf club, which was one positive. Something he could defend himself with.

But there was no more time to think as the Bride's axe nearly took off his head. It sailed past him and hit the minibus with a crunch through its metal.

He ducked out of the way as she swung again, parrying with the golf club, deflecting the next blow, and the one after that. Axe met nine iron with jarring clangs that reverberated through his body. His was no match for her weapon, nor her strength, not with the pain he was in. With each hit, he was pushed further back.

Patrick could *not* let this happen. Not now. Not like this. He had survived a breakdown. Suicidal thoughts. An axe to the leg. This would not beat him.

His face hardened as he screamed at her as loudly and bestially as he could. He locked his fingers around his grip and zoned in on his target.

The Bride paused, confused by his aggression.

With one perfect swing, the golf club connected.

The iron met rancid, bloated flesh. Dark, oily, fizzing blood sprayed across the outside of the minibus. Another hit followed, and the Bride staggered, dazed, then slammed down to the ground.

He didn't wish to savour any moment of victory, he

had seen too many horror films. He knew what happened if you got too smug. Using the nine iron as a crutch, he limped across the car park, needing to get off the open streets, and headed for the path leading towards the gardens.

As he moved, he cast glances towards the shadowed treeline beside him. He could see shadows moving about in the dark. More of them. Many more.

The three attempting femininity had made it to the church door.

Mikey was feeling exhausted, with his hips hurting from all the swaying.

But they were not alone. Julie wasn't far behind.

"Oh, Christ! It's the ex." Mikey said, finally clocking her.

Graham shouted into the walkie-talkie. "Vince. We're outside. Let us in. For *fuck's sake*, open the bloody door!"

Vince and Matt could not hear Graham's pleas. They were too busy, staring at a horror show in a back room of the church. One that had been converted into some kind of mortuary. A mortuary with walls that were now red from blood spray.

A body on the cold metal slab lay in front of them. A woman. She had been opened like a textbook. Her whole body splayed apart, with electrodes dangling from every organ within her body. Cables from inside that fed into broken machines around her.

"Nobody move," Graham said through a fake grin. "Keep smiling."

Outside, the boys were keeping up the act, as Julie stood in front of them. They did not fight, in case the rest of the nearby horde heard. They had to convince her.

There, Julie stood, toe to toe with Mikey, looking directly at him. Her mouth twitched as some recognition plagued her.

She frowned as her lip curled. She felt something deep inside. Beyond her death. In the small part of her that remained. She felt betrayed. Something in her knew him, knew how he broke her heart, and now, how she wanted to eat his in return.

She lunged, grabbed the handbag from his hand, and hurled it across the street.

Mikey's façade broke open, unable to keep up the pretence.

"For *fuck's* sake, Julie. We split up. Get over it!"

The punch from her was instant. A brutal thump, square on the nose. Mikey's legs gave way, and he collapsed. His vision was spinning around him.

Gavin stepped in to attack, but she whirled, lashing out. She caught him on the jaw with one solid hook. Unlike Mikey, though, the impact of her punch had little effect on him.

Immediately, his training kicked in. In a blur of

movement, he got Julie in a headlock and, without a second thought, twisted.

SNAP.

As he let go, she remained standing, neck hanging at a night angle.

Like a headless chicken, her body had not realized what had happened at first, carrying her a few steps to the left before her legs gave way.

She dropped, right at someone's feet.

Patrick had arrived.

He looked up at them breathless, staring at their clothes.

"I am *so* glad to see you gays, I mean guys," he corrected with a laugh.

"Cute," Graham groaned. "Where did you come from?"

"I took the scenic route," Patrick replied as he moaned with pain. "I... I think I gotta..." He broke off mid-sentence, easing himself down onto the steps. The blood from his leg was darker now, thicker, dripping over his shoes.

Inside Bubbles' kitchen, Neil was still tied to the chair, still trying to wriggle free. The ropes creaked the more he moved, but they did not break.

Bubbles paused, mid-bite through the last of his little finger.

She stared, irritated at him moving, and jabbed him

with the tip of the whirring, electric carving knife. It cut through his t-shirt and broke through the skin.

Instead of screaming, Neil started laughing. Hysterically. His brain was clearly circling the drain.

"Owww! What the hell was that?" he laughed again.

Another jab, on his arm this time, cutting him a second time.

"Knock it off! Why don't you just sit on me and get it over with?"

The next stab was a mistake. The blade caught on the rope on his wrist, cutting clean through it, instead of his flesh.

Neil didn't waste the moment.

He sprang to his feet, cackling, wild-eyed. Grabbed the knife out of her hands with his now free hand before she could react.

She lunged at him. But he was faster.

He managed to sidestep her huge arm swinging at him. And as she did, she smashed into the chair freeing the rest of his bindings.

He raised the motorized blade, and drove it deep into her neck.

She reeled, gargling a scream. Her body shuddered as the knife cut through her throat. She collapsed, her bulk smashing through the table, through her finger cake. The knife pulled from Neil's grip, still buzzing in her neck.

Neil was still laughing, staring at her, and around the room. But his eyes were not laughing. They looked tormented.

A minute later, he raced out of the front door like a man launched from a cannon. His trainers skidded on the paving stones as he shot down the garden path, his heart jackhammering in his chest. His mind was spinning with the memories of his recent brush with amateur surgery.

He didn't make it far.

Six of the horde were in front of him. Not wandering. Not moaning. Not hunting. Just standing there, facing away in a line, and in his way.

The Snipper clicked her scissors in beat.

The Chavvie Teenager stood aimlessly with her pigtails askew.

The Lollipop Lady brandished her stop sign, waving it around.

The Barmaid was still applying lipstick now somewhere near her chin.

The Schoolgirl, looking far from innocent, chewed on a severed hand she had found somewhere.

And finally, the Butcher. Massive. Mottled. Murderous.

Their heads all turned to Neil at once, sensing his presence.

"Oh, come *on*!" he moaned. An exasperated, universe-has-it-in-for-me sigh.

Without another word, he ran straight back inside the house he'd just escaped from. He veered straight for the stairs and thundered up, taking the steps two at a time.

And all six women followed him like hounds chasing a rabbit.

Phase Two

The walkie-talkie crackled to life. Graham's voice filtered through the static.

'Vince. Are you taking the piss or what?

From a doorway at the back of the church, Vince and Matt emerged, both unable to process what they had just seen in the mortuary.

'Vince, Matt. Pick up! Pick up! Pick up! Pick up! Open the fucking doors!'

They sprang into action as they ran towards the entrance.

Vince scooped up the walkie-talkie, clicking the talk button.

"Hold on, mate, we're coming."

The heavy church doors creaked as they opened, and Matt ushered them all inside.

"Come on!" he shouted. "Go, go, go!"

He moved back in to make room, only to re-emerge a few moments later, frowning.

No one had moved. Instead, they were all staring into the village at something.

Matt peered out to see what had caught their attention.

There, halfway between them and the car park, like a roofer with a death wish, was Neil.

After climbing through Bubbles' attic skylight, Neil was running across the roof tiles. Crossing from house to house.

The shouts from the church made him come to a stop. He recognized the voices. His friends. Still in one piece. Waving at him.

It was enough to put a spring in his step.

"You beautiful buggers," he grinned.

Jogging across the roof tiles like a Poundland Indiana Jones. Trying his best not to fall, yet having no idea what he was doing.

As he approached the edge of one roof, heading towards the church, he was about to jump to the next, when something caught his eye.

A CCTV camera, mounted on a short pole between two chimneys. Below it, a small speaker. Both branded with a white dolphin logo.

He frowned at it confused. "What the f—"

His foot slipped as the slates moved under his weight. For a terrifying half-second, he teetered at the edge, arms waving around like a cartoon character, keeping his balance.

Thankfully, he righted himself.

From the church steps, the others watched, breath held.

Neil then calculated the gap between the two houses and gave himself a nod.

He carefully stepped back up the roof, giving himself a small run up, before sprinting forward and launching himself into the air.

He soared, in his own mind, at least. Yet, much to the surprise of everyone watching at the church, he made it.

Arms out. Knees bent. Landing like it was an Olympian's dismount.

"That," he shouted triumphantly, "*That* is how we do that!"

And then the roof gave way.

A tremendous crack, followed by an undignified yelp as Neil disappeared in a shower of broken tiles and wooden beams, swallowed whole by the building below.

At the steps of the church, Vince made a move to help Neil, but Gavin blocked him.

"Show's over," he said. "Everyone's gotta get inside, now."

Vince didn't reply. He quickly raised the barrel of his tiny water pistol and pointed it straight at Gavin's nose, as if it were a real gun.

"I don't think so," Vince said.

Neil had fallen through the roof and straight into misfortune, as if fate had taken aim at him.

He didn't land with a *thud* or a *crack*, but with a squelch. Face-first onto a bed, into what remained of a man.

Dust and debris still tumbled around him as Neil scrambled off the corpse, coughing and looking around. He kept his gaze off the man, not wanting to see more than he already had of his grim end, but was met with the gaze of three undead women. All rotten and blotchy.

The one in the middle, the one in full leather corsetry, was obviously a dominatrix. The two flanking her were totally naked.

He was in a brothel.

Neil could not help but let out a chuckle. "Moodley," he said. "You dirty bastards."

The three glared hungrily.

"Alright, ladies," Neil sighed with the cheer of a condemned man. "Who's first?"

Apparently, all of them were.

The Dominatrix pushed forward with authority, but

her companions weren't having it. They snarled and elbowed each other out of the way, jostling for position. What began as an undead sexual threat very quickly devolved into a slap fight with claws between the monsters.

Neil didn't wait to see who won. He rolled off the bed, and made a beeline for the door.

With one hand on the doorknob, he paused and turned back.

"I'll call you, yeah?" he said with a grin, before slipping out into the corridor.

"Stop it, guys," Mikey pleaded, trying to talk sense.

But Gavin still hadn't budged. He eyed Vince's water pistol with bemused disinterest.

"Is that supposed to frighten me?"

"I don't know," Vince nodded sideways at Matt. "He said it would make me feel sexy."

"Does it?"

Vince considered it, briefly. "Yeah. A bit. It does."

Gavin then whipped out his own weapon. Real, steel, and far more convincing, and pointed it squarely back.

"Can we do this male posturing bullshit later?" Graham complained, as if they were arguing over car parking, not having an armed standoff during an undead siege. "You can continue showing each other your dicks inside. Besides, he's already run out of bullets."

Gavin kept his gun aimed, but frowned at the

revelation being shared. "Listen. We're just fast food to these women. Some of us are going to get McFucked if we don't act now. We need to deal with it." His words were tough, but his perfect makeup made it not threatening in the slightest.

Vince, still with toy gun pointed, took out his Zippo, flicked the lid and lit it. He held the flame up to his own barrel with a smile. "You think it's just water in this thing, you prick? Wrong, it's—"

Gavin didn't let him finish, before slapping the lighter out of Vince's hand.

Neil burst out the brothel's front door, bolted across the lawn and made it to the pavement. Glancing back up the street behind him, he saw six figures tumbling out of Bubble's house: the Butcher, the Snipper, the Barmaid, the Chavvie Teenager, the Lollipop Lady, and the Schoolgirl. All headed for him.

With a renewed jolt of fear, he scarpered to the church, up the steps, and through the open door without stopping. All Matt, Mikey, Graham, Vince and Gavin heard was a one-word quip. Aimed at them as he ran by:

"Slags."

The six undead women were relentlessly getting closer to the church. The Snipper was in the lead, her blades twitching, held in front of her.

Snip, snip.

Snip, snip.

Vince, lowering his gun, stared at the zombie's approach as they came to a halt at the bottom of the steps, staring up at them. The Snipper bared her teeth in a bloody snarl.

"Not today, sweetheart," he muttered, hurriedly following Neil inside.

When the women all roared, scampering up the steps toward them, the rest of the men took the cue and ran in.

Getting to the church door as it slammed shut, the Snipper pressed her face against the thick wood and exhaled a furious hiss through her teeth. Her scissors flailed for a few seconds.

Snip, snip.
Snip, snip.

Then, gradually, the snipping slowed to a stop.

Inside, with the large doors locked, it felt almost safe. The thick stone walls had stood for hundreds of years. Even the angriest of the undead outside could not smash their way in with any ease.

The nave was still dark, aside from the glow of the moonlight outside, and the few flickering monitors.

After a few minutes, a lull now settled over them, an exhausted silence.

Gavin had finished changing out of his dress and back into his soldier's overalls. He lingered by one of the tall stained-glass windows, peering out occasionally, then glancing at his watch.

The rest were spread about the church, lying on the floor, sat on the chairs, trying not to notice the bloodstains or bits of people scattered about.

Matt was hunched over a pile of shattered electronics and cables, trying to coax any life out of the ruined command centre.

Neil was on the steps to where the altar had once sat, which was now just a foldaway table. He was cradling a walkie-talkie in one hand, and with the other, stared at the now bandaged stump where his finger used to be.

"I don't think I actually ever used that finger for anything," he said. "I have no idea what it's even for."

The radio crackled. Mikey's voice came through. *'Neil, mate, there's nothing up here.'*

Neil clicked the button. "Well, come back down then."

In one corner, Patrick let out a sharp yelp as Graham yanked a tight bandage around his injured leg.

"Shut up, you girl," Graham said, pulling the fabric tighter out of spite.

Neil looked over. "Talking of girls..."

And right on cue, Mikey walked out from the stairway, still wearing the same ill-fitting miniskirt as before. He handed his walkie-talkie to Graham.

"There's not even a spare choir boy outfit up there," he said with dramatic disappointment. Then added, before heading for the door, "I'm going to get my handbag. She can't have thrown it far."

"Sit down, silly bollocks," Vince yelled from across the room. "You look beautiful just as you are. Besides, they are right out there ready to eat you. You really think it's worth it?"

Mikey sighed, knowing he was right. He dropped into the seat with a sulk.

Neil grinned. "I think that Butcher woman took a shine to you, Mikey. You might be in there."

Mikey sighed. "She's not my type."

"What about one of the others though?" Neil added. "You would, wouldn't you?"

"Do you *ever* have a day off?" Graham said, exasperated.

Neil was undeterred. "There were these three kinky birds in that house back there and, for a second, I thought... y'know, as long as they didn't sick up on me or anything. I could..."

Patrick, who had mostly been preoccupied with not bleeding to death, perked up. "That one with the scissors is pretty fit."

"She'd be wearing your bollocks for earrings before you could buy her a drink," Neil replied.

"I like the one with the axe," Matt offered, eyes still fixed on the tangled wires in front of him.

"She's married," said Mikey and Neil in unison.

Graham groaned, rubbing his temples like someone who'd just walked into the wrong meeting room. "I can't believe I'm hearing this. You people have *zero* respect for women."

Neil waved a dismissive hand. "Come on, Graham.

It's why you bat for the other team, isn't it? All women are mental."

"You can't just make that kind of sweeping generalisation about an entire gender, Neil."

"Why not? Look at us... look at Vince. His glory days are over. His missus did that to him. He was a king when he met her, and she turned him into a ghost."

"In case you've forgotten," Graham snapped, "the reason we brought him out here is so we could convince him that all women are not out to get him."

"Yeah, cheers," Vince added dryly. "That's going really well, innit?" He was perched on the edge of a chair, still held onto the water pistol like it might turn into something useful.

Neil shrugged. "Anyway, none of the things out there *are* women. I have no respect for whatever the fuck they are."

Vince had been watching Gavin for a while now. The man hadn't sat still once. Glancing out windows, tapping his watch, prowling around like a caged animal with combat boots, searching through random crates that lay about.

"Hey Marvin, somewhere you have to be at four in the morning?" Vince said. "Why do you keep checking your watch, eh?"

Gavin didn't even look over. "Why do you keep forgetting my name? I'm the most important person here, for Christ's sake."

"Oh yeah? How do you figure that?"

"Because I'm the only one who knows what's really going on."

That got everyone's attention. The banter immediately died down.

Neil stood. "Well, perhaps you'd like to let us in on the joke, because I'm still waiting for the bloody punchline."

"The joke is: six blokes walk into a village. The poof, the hippy, the scrote, the geek, Jack-the-lad, and the Redundant Leader. The punchline is, and you'll love this... You're all going to die unless you listen to me."

"Did he really just call me a poof?" Graham asked with an exasperated laugh.

Gavin returned to looking through some of the boxes. The insult hung in the air, not quite landing, but not quite fading either.

"So, what are you looking for, G.I. Twat?" Vince asked.

Gavin smiled as he reached into one crate and pulled out something, holding it aloft. A plastic device the size of a large remote control, complete with a gleaming white dolphin logo on one side.

"I'm looking for *this*."

From across the room, Matt's voice rang out. "Okay, done it, I think."

A *snap*. A burst of sparks. The computers shuddered, screens crackled, and—miraculously, they came alive. One by one, CCTV feeds flickered into focus. Rooftop angles. Street corners. Every lane and alley in Moodley could be seen in grainy, monochrome surveillance, and along with it, all the lights in the church came on.

"You bloody marvellous bastard," Patrick smiled.

They all crowded around the screens. Gavin included.

Vince looked at him, then back at the screens. "You've got the whole village under surveillance?"

Before he could answer, the final monitor blinked on. A woman's face appeared. Not one of the undead, not a civilian either. She stared into the camera with a mix of confusion and irritation.

"Well, it's about time!" she grunted, in a clipped, headteacher tone. "You've been offline for over twenty-two hours. Some of us need to sleep, you know?... Now, what's going on? And why was my so-called escort called back to Moodley last night? He took off without a word like someone had lit a rocket under his arse and didn't even bother to unchain the fucking briefcase!"

She raised her arm. A metal briefcase was handcuffed to her wrist.

Matt whispered. "That's Meg Nut."

"The bird from the posters?" Neil asked.

Meg stared through the screen. "Wait, who are you? You're not part of Project Cathouse. Where's the colonel?"

A sharp pop from the monitor, and the screen began to flicker. Meg Nut's angry words suddenly cut off, as all the feeds flickered and died, taking the lights above with them. Again leaving the church in a half-darkness.

And like a final point to the moment, Meg's monitor burst into flames.

"Get her back!" Neil shouted.

Matt motioned to the screen. "It's on fire, Neil, this isn't a coding error."

Vince turned to Gavin, face lit by the glow of the fire. "Now tell us, what the fuck is Project Cathouse?"

Gavin's watch started beeping. He ignored the question and turned to the window with a scared look on his face.

Outside, the Snipper had stopped mid-stride. Her scissors hung slack by her side. Her head started to twitch violently. She opened her mouth and started vomiting a thicker, darker mud-like sludge down the front of her blouse. And as she did, she spasmed, remaining upright, jerking, contorting.

"It's happening," Gavin said, worried.

Vince joined him at the window, looked at Gavin's still beeping watch, then outside. "Right on time, by the sounds of your watch," he said. "Now you gonna tell us what's happening?"

Gavin didn't turn around. "Phase Two."

Outside, across Moodley and into the woods, all the undead convulsed, vomiting the same thick sludge. They had started at the same time, and one by one began to hit the ground in fits, their contortions getting too violent to keep them upright.

Only Bad Candy remained still. Sitting in the

minibus, she peered through the window like a curious zombie child. Her gaze was locked on the Bride, who now contorted outside, her head thrashing, spewing sludge for what seemed like an age.

Then she stopped, but only for a minute...

Her eyes opened again, but they were not the same. There were no pupils, no whites. Just a deep, unsettling black, like the eyes of a shark.

Neil was trying to understand.

"Hold on a bloody minute," he said. "If this is Phase Two, what the hell was Phase One?"

"Sickness. Disorientation. Psychosis," Gavin replied, calm and resigned. "Phase Two is the mutation. The next level."

"Mutation into what?" Vince asked.

Gavin stared down at his feet as he spoke, realizing he had no more reason to cover this up anymore. "Until now, their behaviour's been aggressive, but totally random. Running on instinct... Well, that's about to change. They're going to get smarter... and faster... Think of them in Phase One as toddlers. Now they are becoming adults."

Back on the steps, the Snipper got to her feet and spat out a mouthful of teeth.

· · ·

"And they are going to get a lot... weirder," Gavin added.

A screech tore through the air from outside. Everyone in the church flinched. Neil stepped forward, shoved Gavin aside, and peered out of the window.

"Oh fucking hell," he said.

The Bride was coming at them in the distance. Her silhouette glowed in the moonlight, as she ran down the street to the church. Her arms, once merely arms, were now tipped with what looked like jagged bony spikes reaching forward like large pincers. She moved differently than before. Not with the random shamble of the walking dead, but with deliberate, scuttering, like a scorpion.

At the top of the steps, the Snipper turned to look back at the window. Her jaw had now elongated. Her mouth a nest of razor-sharp teeth, as a long, black serpentine tongue flicked through them, tasting the air.

She took a breath in and looked up to the sky, making that screeching call.

On the street, the Butcher responded, rising slowly from the ground. Her mass was much larger now, almost eight feet tall and just as wide. Her hair had fallen out and her skin was also harder, like it had been callused from head to foot with a tough armour. She replied to the Snipper's call with her own guttural shriek.

. . .

Neil was pale, and looked horrified as he backed away from the window.

"Lads?" he said, weakly. "The battle of the sexes just got a lot uglier."

The screeching outside got louder, as the mutated undead all started to join in the same chorus.

"What are they doing?" Vince asked.

"What do you think?" Gavin replied. "They're talking to each other, and shouting at us,"

Neil gave a snort, trying to push aside his nerves. "Great. They're giving us lip now."

A crash sounded from the door, where outside, the Bride had slammed her axe into the wood.

Gavin reached for the button on the remote, but Vince was faster, grabbing his wrist just in time, stopping the button being pressed.

"What is that, then?" Vince asked, motioning to the remote.

"It's called the Dolphin," Gavin relented. "High-frequency sonic deterrents are set up all over the village, all linked to a console here in the church. Emits a painful sound that only women can hear. This remote activates it."

Patrick was angry. "There was a failsafe all along, and you *knew* about it? You could have—"

"It only works after Phase Two," Gavin interrupted.

"Stop bleeding talking about it," Neil said, "and press the bloody button."

Vince let go of Gavin's wrist.

He pushed the button.

They stood in silence, waiting for a few seconds.

"Is it working?" Graham asked.

"I dunno," Neil replied. "Can *you* hear it?"

Graham flipped him the middle finger.

Another *thunk* at the door. The Bride's axe struck the church again.

"Well, that proves it" Mikey sighed. "It doesn't work, does it?"

"Nope," said Vince. "There's a surprise, eh?"

Gavin looked at the remote, rattled. "This isn't bloody funny. They'll be relentless now. They'll hunt in packs. We're totally and completely *fucked*."

"Hunt what?" asked Neil. "Hunt us?"

Gavin nodded, as he broke out in a sweat. "You must know how this works by now. The female... Hunts... The male."

"I blame you for this, Neil," Patrick pointed accusingly. "This is your bad karma come back to bite us all on the arse."

Neil wasn't listening. Instead, he walked over to Gavin, pushing him with his good hand. The soldier, caught off-guard, stumbled until his back hit the confessional booth.

"For the sake of clarity," Neil said, "we're not just dealing with a few insane women anymore, right? What you boys have created here is an army of pissed-off, man-hating, cannibal feminists."

"Now, Marvin, just tell us, what the *hell* is Project Cathouse?" Vince added.

"*Gavin*, My fucking name is Gavin. Not Marvin.

Not Martin. Not Gerald. Not Kevin. Gavin. G. A. V. I. N. *Gavin*!" he snapped.

Everyone was silenced by the outburst.

He took a breath and continued. "Look, you don't understand. We've got a biological weapon that can turn half the population against the other. No armies. No tanks. Just... infection. It's a perfect weapon, in theory..."

"It's going to put you out of a job then," Patrick quipped, though he found none of this funny.

Gavin hesitated as the realisation struck him. He had not even considered that possibility.

Vince pressed on with his interrogation. "So, what is this? A test run? You set the virus loose in an isolated village like Moodley, you get the beers in and watch it all on CCTV. That sound about right?"

"They did this kind of thing in America in the fifties," Matt said. "LSD experiments on the population. Even on soldiers."

Mikey pointed to one of the campaign posters on the wall. "What's Meg Nut got to do with it?"

Gavin shook his head. "She's just the delivery."

"Delivering what?" Patrick asked.

Matt was already prying open one of the wooden crates, hoping to find weapons, when he stared down at the contents, confused.

"What do you think?" Gavin raised his voice. "How *stupid* are you people?"

Mikey looked up, puzzled. "Why is this filled with boxes of Wundawash?" But his voice was lost among the others shouting.

Gavin was shaking his head. "How can you not be getting this?"

"Just spit it out," Vince said. "For Christ's sake, Gareth."

"For the last time, my FUCKING NAME IS MARVIN!"

"I thought he said it was Gavin?" Neil asked quietly.

Crack!

A white cloud of Wundawash detergent exploded from out of the box, as Matt ripped open its lid. Covering himself in powder.

Everyone turned.

"I get it now," Matt said. "The virus is in the soap powder, right?"

They turned back to Gavin.

"It's biological," he continued. "They made it so it bursts out of the package when opened. Basic but quite genius really. Meg Nut gave free boxes away, claiming it was a sponsorship, and all the housewives took one."

"And you then poisoned them all?" Graham said, disgusted. "You should be ashamed... What have you got to say for yourself?"

There was a pause, Gavin shrugged, then—

"Arg!" he croaked loudly. His eyes bulged, before he collapsed forward onto the floor with a heavy thud, still clutching the remote. His back had been sliced open, spine cut in two, as blood gushed up into the air like a small fountain.

Behind him, stood in the confessional booth, was what had once been a sweet old lady. But there was nothing sweet here now. Her cardigan was soaked in brown lumpy bile. Her teeth were sharp like small brown knives. Her back was split from neck to arse, and a line of bony spikes poked through.

In her hand, she held a glinting pair of garden shears, wet with Gavin's blood.

"Get back!" Vince shouted. "Everybody get back!"

Everyone did, except for Mikey.

Vince fired the water pistol, spurting nitro fuel into her face.

"Vince, don't," Mikey pleaded. "Leave it out, mate..." He stared at the old lady with tears in his eyes. "It's my Nan."

"I thought she was on a cruise?" Vince asked.

"So did I!"

She turned to Mikey and opened her mouth wider.

"Oh man," he whimpered. "She's foaming at the bloody mouth."

"Don't look at her," Patrick said.

But it was too late.

Nan lunged, snipping wildly with her shears at Vince, making him back away. But he was not her focus of attention. Mikey was.

Mikey was too scared and upset to move.

As she raised her shears, ready to cut at Mikey's neck —*Thwack*.

Matt had run forward, Patrick's nine iron in his hand, and smashed it into Nan's skull. Sending her crashing back into the confessional.

He ran over and hit her with it again.

Thwack.

Then again.

Thwack.

And again.

Thwack.

And again.

Thwack.

Blood sprayed through the air, coating him as he battered her small grey, yet monstrous head in. Bits of viscera and brain flew out, sticking to his clothes, as her head was battered into nothing.

Thwack.

Thwack.

Thwack.

Thwack.

Matt then stopped, covered in Mikey's nan. His eyes were wide, and the nine iron tightly gripped in his hand.

"You got some stuff on your face, mate," Neil said, unhelpfully.

Matt then dropped the club and walked off slowly towards the back of the nave, to the back room. He needed a moment alone.

"Matt?" Vince called. "Are you okay?"

No reply, as he went through the back room door, letting it close behind him.

"Leave him," Neil said. "Poor bugger's traumatised."

"I think *I'm* traumatised after that," Patrick raised his shaky hand, showing them.

"You? *I'm* the one who's fucking traumatised!" Mikey shouted. "Look what he did to my Nan!"

Neil sniffed, changing the subject. "Can anyone else smell bacon?"

Vince shook his head and went to follow Matt.

Opening the back room door, Vince looked in.

"Matt, mate?" he said.

The whole room reeked of scorched flesh.

"You alright?"

The door on the other side of the room, leading to the makeshift mortuary, was open.

"What d'you go in there for?" Vince asked. "Come on, let's talk about this."

As he walked into the mortuary, expecting to see Matt crouched in a corner having an emotional moment, he gasped.

Matt was not sat, but dangled helplessly in the Goth Witch's grasp, her charred fingers gripping his throat. Smoke drifted around her, as her flesh burned from the inside out. Her skin was cracking and showed the inferno beneath. She was into Phase Two now, and the fire that consumed her was now a part of her... In her other hand she still held her sword.

Her one good eye, now all black, stared at Vince.

Matt didn't struggle. He couldn't. But his eyes, wide and full of terrified clarity, met Vince's across the room. There was no plea for help. Only the awful, dawning certainty of what was about to happen. Something neither of them could stop.

With a sudden thrust, the Goth Witch drove her

sword clean through Matt's stomach, and up through his chest, into his head, and out of the top of his skull.

And then, almost mockingly, she twisted the blade. Ripping apart all of Matt's insides. Churning and demolishing them.

Her gaze never left Vince.

He ran back with a scream, slamming the door behind him. He raced back into the nave, where everyone had come over, after hearing the noise.

Neil saw the look in his eyes. "What happened? Is he alright?"

"No," Vince replied hollowly. "That eye-patched twat—"

The tip of the sword pierced through the storeroom door, right next to Vince. He rushed away as the Goth Witch pulled her sword out and hacked through the handle. Crashing her way into the room.

"She fucking done him with that sword!" Vince shouted.

Mikey, deep in grief about his nan, could not take this added bad news. A quiet pop in his mind, like a lightbulb shorting out, forced him to shout out.

"Fuck you!" he screamed as he broke into a sprint towards the Goth Witch, throwing himself at her with reckless abandon. His charge drove her back through the storeroom and back into the mortuary.

The others froze for a moment, stunned. Then, fuelled by rage, fear, adrenaline, or just misplaced peer pressure, they ran after him.

. . .

The mortuary now was a vision of violence. The Goth Witch moved like a whirlwind, sword slashing, fists flying, as Mikey had straddled her, headbutting her burning face again and again.

As she managed to toss him aside, Patrick punched her in the kidneys. In reply, she kicked him into a stack of autopsy trays.

Vince was next. In return for a kick in the gut, she yanked him by the hair and hurled him into a gurney. It smashed into a wall.

A monitor crashed to the ground.

Screams mingled with the clatter of broken equipment and the shrieks of pure savagery.

The dead bodies in here acted like landing pads for every living thing that was being hurled around.

In the melee, the sword was dropped.

Mikey's eyes lit up as he grabbed it.

He quickly raised it above his head. It was not light. The Goth Witch had made it look easy to wield.

Everyone moved back. No one wanted to get in the way of him.

Mikey swung hard, once... twice... and on the third swing the blade met its target. Right across her belly. Blood, guts and dark sludge fountained. The Goth Witch fell, and when she did Mikey stood over her, driving the blade through her chest and into the floor.

Everyone stared at Mikey as he panted, blood-covered, still shaking.

He then dropped the sword.

They turned, slowly, to look at Matt's body. He was

slumped in the corner, his body hollowed out by the attack.

"Shit," Patrick breathed, catching sight of Matt, hollowed out and slumped in a corner. He tried not to cry. "Look at the state of him."

"We can't leave him like this," Graham said.

"What? In a mortuary?" Neil said. Four looks shot daggers in his direction. "Sorry, sorry," he added quickly. "I'm just as freaked out as the rest of you."

A noise interrupted the moment. A sound that came from their left, beyond an archway that led to a dark, adjoining room. A high-pitched noise. One that was too far away to determine what it was.

With frayed nerves, they cautiously followed the sound.

Beyond the archway, in the darkness, there was a large metal door, half open, swaying in the light breeze that came from beyond it. The door was marked *Service Access* by a hanging sign above its frame.

Vince approached first, pulling the water pistol from his belt. He peered through, expecting the worst.

Ahead, steps led down into the darkness.

"We can't go down there," Neil said. "That's how she got in."

Behind, from the church door, they could still hear the Bride's axe crash into the wood, reminding them of the narrowing odds of their escape.

Vince swallowed, hating what he was about to say. "This could be the only way we're going to get out."

No one wanted to agree, but no one wanted to be

here when the front door would eventually be smashed in, even if they were heading towards a noise that could be worse than everything else.

They descended the steps slowly, and stone soon gave way to a metal grated flooring.

They found themselves in a long, grimy access tunnel.

Unlike upstairs, there was still electricity down here. Small lights lined the curved ceiling, though they pulsed weakly and lit very little. Still, they glowed enough to reveal smears of blood across the walls. On the metal floor sat chunks of meat. Bits of what used to be people.

They slowly carried on. Huddled.

Until, up ahead, they noticed a light coming from around the corner. Much brighter than in here. Shining out like a beacon.

"What the hell is that?" Graham whispered, pointing to the light.

"Probably a room full of murderous monsters," Neil joked, but his smile never appeared.

They turned the corner.

"Oh, bollocks," they all said, as if rehearsed.

The tunnel had opened into a wide, concrete-lined room lit by failing bulbs. In the centre of it lay an enormous pile of human remains.

Patrick, Neil, Mikey and Vince stared in horror at what was a mountain of men. Devoured. Decapitated. Gutted and discarded.

"It's the missing half of Moodley," Vince said.

Graham turned away, trying to hold down whatever was in his stomach. "Oh God. It's all the men. Every single one."

"Parts of them, anyway," Neil added.

"Oh fuck no." Patrick stepped forward. "No, no, no."

"What?" Vince asked.

"It's a nest," he said, almost not believing it. "We are in their *fucking* nest! That pile is their food. They just kill and drag them down here, ready to feast."

A high-pitched squeal echoed from deeper within the room. Forcing them to shut up.

Behind the pile of body parts, something appeared.

The Schoolgirl, crawling on all fours, scurried over the corpses. Her mouth dripped red, as between her teeth, she bit on a severed arm.

From the far side of the room, the Barmaid also crawled into view. She saw the Schoolgirl's dangling prize and lunged at it. Sinking her sharp teeth into its other end. These two monsters then began a gruesome tug-of-war, as they snarled at each other over the meat.

The men didn't move. They *couldn't* move. They were too afraid to make a sound.

Then another figure entered from the far side of the nest. Not crawling, not skittish, but calm and unhurried.

The Foxhunter. Still with a golf ball wedged in her eye socket.

She was dragging Julie's limp body behind her, her feet squelching as she stood on all the remains. She didn't even glance at the men. She just let out a high-pitched shriek as she entered. The same noise they had heard from the mortuary.

They didn't need to be told twice, as Vince motioned to fall back, which they all did, as quietly as they could.

They moved fast into the tunnel, heading back to the church.

They all ducked under a low-hanging pipe, except Patrick, who, limping at the rear, misjudged the height and *clang!* smashed his head against it. The sound rang out like a bell, reverberating throughout the entire network.

In the nest, the Foxhunter's head turned. As it did, her golf ball eye popped loose and dangled on a strip of sinew from her ruined eyeball below. It swung like a wet pendulum across her face.

She snarled.

Patrick rubbed his sore head as the shriek sounded significantly closer.

They turned, and there, with the light from the nest flickering behind them, stood the Foxhunter, the Schoolgirl, and the Barmaid, all rushing towards them. Hungry and angry.

The men turned and ran back up the steps into the church.

Vince slammed the door behind them. It might have been metal, but it bounced uselessly against its frame. There was no lock, let alone a latch.

"That was productive," Neil said.

There was no time to argue. They bolted again, backing out through the mortuary and into the back room. They got out into the nave just in time to see the front doors crack inward.

Walking in was the Bride. Axe in hand. The second time she had walked down here in a week.

From outside, the shrieks and roars of others could be heard, thundering up the steps to join them.

"There!" Vince shouted, pointing to the staircase.

As they disappeared upstairs, the Snipper and the Bride stormed down the aisle after them. They were soon met by the Foxhunter, the Schoolgirl and the Barmaid, who came out from the back room.

They did not pause as they grouped together and followed up the staircase.

The landing door opened as Vince, Neil, Mikey, Patrick and Graham ran in.

Vince paused next to an emergency fire hose that was coiled on the wall.

"Neil!" he called out. "Turn this thing on!" He

yanked the hose up from its reel, and aimed it down the stairs. "Let's flush 'em out."

Neil found and immediately spun the valve.

Expecting a huge torrent, the hose just shuddered. Wheezing as it let out a single, pathetic dribble.

"This is almost fucking poetic," Neil sighed.

Vince frantically shook the nozzle. More drips came out. Nothing else.

"Put it away, mate," Neil added. "You're firing blanks."

Down the stairs, the monsters surged upward. The Snipper leading, teeth out and scissors snipping.

Snip, snip.

Snip, snip.

Vince dropped the hose, and they ran once more.

They rushed into the Vicar's study, shutting the door, and started to barricade it. Shoving a bookshelf over. But that was not enough. Chairs, tables, anything they could grab was heaped onto the pile to stop the door from opening.

Vince looked around the room. There were no exits. Just a single window.

Hurrying over, he saw that it led out onto the flat roof, and tried to open it. It was their only route out. But it was stuck.

"Neil, give me a hand," he called back.

Together, within moments, they had forced the window open, just enough for them to squeeze through.

. . .

Out in the middle of village, the streets had gone quiet again.

A lone figure wandered across the car park. Whistling to himself as he cracked open a can of beer. One that he had been waiting all night to drink.

It was Banksy.

He had finally made it to Moodley.

Escape

Inside the minibus, Bad Candy stirred. Her ears twitched at the hiss of a beer can popping outside. She crept to the window, pressing her face against the glass, snarling as her fingers clawed at the pane, watching Banksy stroll by. Oblivious and carefree.

He crossed the car park and wandered down the street, humming to himself. Nothing seemed out of place, not even the fact that the entrance to the village had been blocked by a collapsed billboard, forcing him to climb through the trees.

It wasn't until he stood in front of the burnt-out toy shop that something finally felt... off.

"Hello?" he called out. "Anybody there?"

He strolled past Bubbles' house.

He could not see in the darkness, but she lay behind the garden wall, motionless, until his voice roused her.

"Hello?" He called out again, walking on.

Bubbles sat up, blood still pouring from her neck wound. She clutched the electric knife in her hand and watched him walk off.

She looked the same as she had before, seemingly late to Phase Two. But as she stood up, ready to run after Banksy, it hit her.

She convulsed, vomited sludge and collapsed again.

As Banksy passed the church, he heard something. A crash of furniture.

He trundled up the steps, still drinking his beer.

When he got to the top, something glinted at him in the moonlight. It was Vince's Zippo, lying on the concrete. As he picked it up, Banksy noticed the hacked-up church door.

He wasn't scared or worried by what he was seeing. He was just confused... that was Banksy all over.

Above, on a flat part of the church roof, Vince and Neil squeezed through the window in the Vicar's study. They scurried to the edge of the roof, looking for an escape route.

Banksy saw them before they had a chance to look down.

"What are you soggy tarts doing up there?"

"Banksy?" Neil gasped. "What time d'you call this?"

"You would not *believe* the shit day I've had."

"You don't know the half of it, mate," Vince muttered, holding up his bandaged hand.

"What's going on anyway?" Banksy asked, sipping his beer. "What's up on the roof?"

"There's a ladder around the corner at Mikey's nan's place," Vince shouted. "Go get it. Don't ask questions. Just hurry!"

Banksy shrugged and wandered off, before turning back.

"Where is the house? I've never been here before."

Vince pointed to the side road behind him. "Go down there, small house with scaffolding outside. You can't miss it."

A loud *thunk* sounded from within the study. It was the Bride's axe, starting to hack through the door.

Vince ran back over and climbed inside, leaving Neil waiting.

Graham and Mikey were pressed against the barricade. The pile shook with each axe blow from the hallway outside.

Vince joined them, pushing his whole weight against the wood. "I'll hold this. Mikey, you get your arse out there."

"It's alright. I've got it," he replied, not moving.

"Michael, get the hell outside!" Vince snapped in full dad-mode.

As Neil helped him outside, Mikey's short skirt rode up high.

"I can see your bikini line from here."

Mikey turned and saw Banksy's head poking up over the roofs edge. "Banksy? What the fuck?"

"What's with the frock?" Banksy said, with a big grin on his face.

Neil wasn't laughing. "What are you doing?" He shouted over.

"Vince said get the ladder."

"So we can get down, you *plank*, not so *you* can get up."

Patrick climbed out of the window next, his leg still throbbing as it bled.

Banksy, still on top of the ladder, stared in amusement like this was all some kind of elaborate prank.

"Did I miss a ruck, Pat? What happened?"

Mikey walked over as he explained. "All the women have gone evil, one of them ate Neil's finger, Matt killed my Nan with a nine iron, and now he's dead and we need to get down the sodding ladder. Okay?"

Banksy didn't say another word as he climbed back down the ladder. "Have you lot been taking drugs or something?"

Mikey climbed down after him, as Patrick and Neil waited to follow.

Before Banksy got near to the ground, something brushed against his foot.

It was the Butcher.

"Go back up! Go back up!" he shouted in a panic, kicking her off.

She lunged, sinking her teeth into his calf.

He tried to scramble up the ladder, pushing against Mikey, who was now pushing Neil.

But the Butcher yanked at the bottom rungs, and the whole ladder started to tip.

Pulled up by Patrick, Neil managed to get back onto the roof, and turned to grab Mikey's hand, but he wasn't fast enough. The ladder tilted, pulling away from the building.

Banksy and Mikey fell to the left, not onto the ground, but onto the next rooftop, landing on the tiles in a heap. Mikey was quick to rush back over and pull the ladder up, out of the grip of the Butcher below.

Banksky held his leg, gasping in pain. "What the fuck was that?" he shouted.

On the church roof, Vince popped his head out of the window.

"What are you doing back up here?" he shouted to Neil.

"Wishing I wasn't."

Just then, the ladder reappeared, laid flat between two rooftops.

Mikey had built a bridge.

"Come on!" he called out.

Patrick was the first to cross. Crawling across unsteadily, but making it over quickly.

Neil was next to crawl across the rungs. As he got halfway across, he looked down and his stomach fell.

Below, the Butcher had been joined by the Foxhunter, the Schoolgirl, and the Barmaid. The four of them clawed up like wild animals, growling and snapping, trying to reach them above, but they were a couple of feet too short.

Graham was still bracing the barricade with his back. He could feel the door heaving with every axe hack behind the door. Across the room, Vince was already halfway out the window.

"Graham. Come on, lad!" he called back.

"Go! I'm right behind you,"

The hacking continued.

As Vince crawled out of the window, everyone was watching him from the other roof. All except Neil, who was looking back into the village.

"Fuck me!" he muttered.

At first, only he noticed, but Patrick soon followed Neil's gaze and his mouth fell open. "Okay, that is... horrible."

Bubbles had returned.

Or what *used* to be Bubbles.

She was now deep into Phase Two.

She thundered down the street, her body grotesquely swollen, warped by the mutation. Her skin seemed to have grown at a greater rate than the rest of her and now sagged and hung off her, fluttering behind like fleshy tendrils in the wind. The mass she had gained shredded her clothes, so now she was naked, monstrous, and storming towards them like a charging bull.

Her rotting flesh rolled and jiggled with each pounding step. Her arms flailed like clubs, and her face, though barely human, still held the same gormless rage.

Everyone on the rooftop stared down at her, speechless, as she ran into the church.

Vince was halfway across the ladder when he turned and shouted as loud as he could.

"Graham, he called out. "Something worse than the Pamplona bull run is coming straight for ya, mate. Run like a bastard and don't look back!"

Graham finally got his nerve together and let go of the barricade.

As he raced to the window, it collapsed behind him in an explosion of splinters.

With a cacophonous crash, Bubbles burst into the room, her bulk ripping the door off its hinges and completely demolishing the barricade.

Coming in behind her, the Bride had stood aside as Bubbles had broken on through.

Graham managed to squeeze himself out the window and land on the roof.

But as he did, a large fleshy hand reached out, as Bubbles grabbed his ankle, dragging him back into the room.

The lads on the roof watched in horror.

Graham kicked at her with everything he had, managing to break free as he broke her fingers with the heel of his shoe.

He got up and sprinted towards the ladder bridge. Quickly falling to his knees, he started crawling across in a panic. As he moved, the whole ladder rocked under his weight.

Everyone was focused on him getting across when Bubbles came smashing through the window, taking half the wall with her.

"Hurry up," Vince called out in a panic.

Graham was nearly there.

"Give me your hand." Vince shouted, reaching out. But they were still too far apart.

Bubbles bounded over to the ladder and grabbed one end of it. The whole thing wobbled, then tipped sideways, as she cast it to one side with ease.

"*No!*" they all screamed, as Graham fell.

As he landed on the patch of grass below, right in the centre of the waiting pack, the wind knocked out of him. He struggled to breathe, gasping, but within seconds, they were on him.

Then one was *literally* on him, as Bubbles hurled herself off the roof ledge.

She landed on Graham with a wet crunch that silenced everyone. Smothering him with her fleshy bulk.

Vince looked down, shaking with shock. He could barely comprehend what he was seeing, one of his mates swallowed by a mound of flesh, then swarmed by screeching monsters. All coming within minutes of another mate getting skewered by a sword.

As Bubbles moved off Graham's limp body, she growled at the others, forcing them to back up as she grabbed his ankle and dragged him off, down the alley, into the shadows.

Rage began to replace Vince's grief as—

Snip, snip.

His gaze shot up to the sound, a furious fire in his eyes.

On the rooftop opposite, the Snipper stood tall, looking directly at them. Her scissors clicked together.

Snip, snip.

She was taunting him.

But he didn't give in. Instead, he turned, looking for a weapon. Seeing one of the dolphin logo CCTV cameras on the side of the chimney, he walked over, tore it off the bricks, and hurled it at her.

It sailed over the gap and shattered just short of her feet. She didn't move. She just kept snipping.

Snip, snip.

Snip, snip.

"Come on then!" he screamed.

The others looked at him with a mixture of shock and sorrow. No one spoke until Neil finally stepped forward and said quietly, "Vince... we've got to go."

Banksy was there, no idea what was happening, but too concerned with his bleeding calf.

Without another word, they turned and retreated along the rooftops.

Behind the butcher's shop, they found a drainpipe and, one by one, began sliding down.

Banksy went first, descending too quickly. His injured leg gave out, and he hit the pavement hard, landing on his backside with a grunt.

Vince followed. As he swung over the edge, he did not notice his Zippo slip from his jacket and clatter to the ground. Once down, he reached over to help Banksy to his feet.

Neil came next, landing with ease before turning to assist Patrick. As Patrick reached the bottom, he spotted the Zippo on the ground and picked it up. Digging into his pocket, he pulled out a slightly bent cigar, one he'd been saving for the weekend, one he suddenly wanted. The stress was getting so great, he needed *something*.

He placed the cigar between his lips and spoke softly, "Sun's coming up soon. Maybe they'll turn back into normal women in the daylight?" He gave a hopeful smile and flicked the Zippo open.

Before he could light it, Neil snatched the lighter from his hand. "You may be right..." he said. "All the screaming and biting usually goes out the window in the morning."

"Banksy," Vince said, holding out his hand. "Give me your phone."

"I left it at home," Banksy shrugged.

Vince shook his head. "Right. Because that would just be too easy, wouldn't it? Where are you parked?"

"There's a huge billboard that fell over, I had to park on the other side of it." Banksy looked at everyone. "Guys, what is going on. What was that woman who bit me?"

"Mutant zombie, mate," Neil replied. "Vince, thoughts of what the fuck we do?"

Vince nodded, choosing the simplest option. "We're going to run there... One at a time. Careful. Quiet."

Naturally, with this group, they listened but didn't follow to the letter.

They all charged at once across the street, over the grass, and up the verge leading to the car park. They ran straight past the minibus and crawled through the trees to the other side of the fallen billboard.

"What the hell was *that*?" Vince's voice rose in annoyance, then dropped, as he realized where they were. "I said *one* at a time, not everyone all at once like a bunch of twats!"

No one bothered to reply as they then saw it. Their escape vehicle.

On the other side of the road was Banksy's car. Or rather, his Smart Car. A two-seater that was parked on the other side.

"Oh, shit! It's a rental. I forgot," Banksy said, realizing the issue.

Vince slowly turned to him. "What do you mean, 'It's a rental'? Where's your van?"

"It broke down. I totally forgot."

Vince sneered, "You *forgot*?"

"Repeating everything I say isn't going to help," Banksy replied.

"I'll tell you what isn't going to help," Vince said. "That fucking moon buggy."

Patrick spoke up, trying to be optimistic. "Maybe we can all squeeze in. I'll sit on someone's lap."

"You're not sitting on my lap," Neil quipped.

"Forget it," Vince said. "It's too small." He turned to Banksy. "I don't even know how *you* got in it."

Banksy looked genuinely offended. "What are you trying to say?"

"This trip was a bad idea," Mikey moaned.

"No? *Really*?" Neil exclaimed sarcastically.

"Look, it could be worse," Banksy offered.

"Could be worse? Neil shouted. "How many fingers am I holding up? They are fucking eating us!"

"I got bit too," Banksy weakly interjected.

Neil continued. "How much worse do you want it to get? Matt? Gone. Graham? Gone! How do—"

Patrick, never one to be left out of an emotional breakdown, cut in.

"Everyone shut up! You think cracking skulls open with a nine iron is my idea of a golfing holiday? Because it's not! But this isn't Mikey's fault. And it isn't Banksy's fault. And it sure as fucking shit isn't my fault. Now... We must work together to facilitate some kind of positive escape scenario because I am not going to die in the shit hole that is fucking Moodley! Now let's move before they catch us."

That is precisely when the Snipper struck.

She came bursting through the billboard like she had been waiting for a dramatic entrance. She lunged at Patrick with both scissors held high, and drove both pairs straight into his chest. Slicing through his heart and lungs like he was made of warm butter. He flew backward towards the Smart Car. But she didn't stop there. She was so fast, she was almost a blur as her arms pumped like a machine, stabbing into Patrick over and over, turning his torso into a cratered mess.

He collapsed onto the car, the tiny bonnet doing nothing to cradle his weight. The Snipper clung on, relentless, continually stabbing.

The rest barely had time to think before the Butcher joined the fray. She swung wide with a cleaver, the blade whistling past them.

Banksy, Vince, Mikey and Neil scattered, screaming as they bolted for the minibus.

Behind them, the Butcher reached for Patrick's corpse, now hanging gracelessly half off the Smart Car's bonnet. She snarled at the Snipper, who hissed back, both eager to claim the bloody prize.

As they fought, Patrick hit the road with a wet thump. His iPod jolted under his weight. A chipper little voice burst out of his headphones, tinny and oblivious.

'Don't worry. There's nothing wrong with you that can't be fixed with a smile.'

. . .

By the minibus, things were getting worse, as if that were possible.

The Phase Two horde were trudging up the street towards them.

"Get on the bus!" Neil shouted as he reached it first, yanking the door open.

He had totally forgot who was in there.

Bad Candy.

She leapt from the shadows, fire poker raised. She shrieked as she flew at him.

"Ruth, no!" Vince cried out, throwing himself in the way.

For a fraction of a second, she hesitated. Her name being called hit her somewhere deep. Behind the gore and insanity, something twitched.

But it was enough time for them to get an advantage.

Vince and Neil jumped her. Wrestling the fire poker away.

Mikey saw his chance and sprinted past the chaos and onto the minibus.

He turned to see Banksy, puffing, gasping, lumbering behind. He wasn't fast enough. The Barmaid was upon him like a tidal wave. She drove the broken Stella bottle into his chest. It dug right through his heart.

Banksy looked down in horror as she let go. The bottleneck jutted out of him, as blood sloshed up inside the glass. It filled the bottle head up until, with a grotesque little pop, the cap burst off the end and crimson poured out like a celebration.

Banksy fell face first and didn't get up again.

"No!" Mikey screamed from the other side of the glass.

Neil finally managed to wrench the poker free from Bad Candy's grip and cracked her across the skull with it. Down she went. Out cold.

He then turned, eyes gleaming, poker ready for more battle, but Vince grabbed him and shoved him onto the minibus.

There was no time for heroics. Not anymore.

The door hissed shut as Vince collapsed into the driver's seat.

Outside, the horde was closing in. Neil, Mikey and Vince could see them fanning out, surrounding the vehicle. Clawing at the bodywork as they hungered to get in.

Vince let his head fall back against the headrest, fingers trembling slightly as they reached into his top pocket. Out came the cigar Neil had handed him earlier. Along with it came the photo. *That* photo.

His wife. His *ex*-wife. Smiling up at him like nothing had changed. As if she weren't the reason his life had been ruined, even before Moodley.

He shoved the cigar between his teeth, and fumbled through his jacket and trousers, looking for a lighter.

The minibus shuddered violently as the horde started

to rock it. Greasy smears trailed down the windows as they clawed and pushed. Some screamed, some vomited bile onto the bodywork. All wanted them dead.

"Come on, Vince. Let's *go*," Mikey shouted, clinging to his armrest. "What are you doing?"

Vince, teeth clenched around the unlit cigar, didn't flinch. "Having a mid-life crisis."

"What? Right now? Can't it wait?"

"Nope."

Neil, hunched behind the passenger seat, chuckled bitterly. "Well, it's about fucking time."

Vince turned his head slightly. "You seen my lighter?"

Neil dug into his pocket. Out came the Zippo. "Try to look after it this time." He tossed it over.

Vince caught it and lit up.

The flame flared, and he inhaled on the cigar.

Outside, the woman snarled and drooled desperately.

He turned to Neil and Mikey, inhaling a lungful before speaking. "You know," he said, suddenly calmer, "I always thought you two were completely fucking useless." He nodded at Neil. "*You* follow your dick around like it's a compass..." Then to Mikey. "...and you're letting your marriage slip through your fingers. Neither one of you knows *anything* about women. And if so, how come you're both still alive?"

Mikey was unable to stop his shaking. "We're not going to be alive for much longer if you don't stop yapping and get us out of here."

Vince ignored him. Looked again at the photo of his wife, once comforting, now just a reminder of his failure.

"The rest of us do everything by the book and *we're* the ones who get shafted." He let that statement hang for a moment, before continuing. "We become exactly what *they* want us to be. Reliable. Mature. Domesticated. And what happens? They get bored, that's what happens. If all women really want is a pet, why don't they just buy a fucking Labrador?"

With the Zippo lit again, he held the photo to the flame. It caught quickly, charring black along the edge of his ex-wife's smile.

His gaze then fell to the lighter itself. The picture of the paw print engraving on it. A gift from his ex... She had called him 'her little puppy', and now it made him feel furious.

He let the burning photo and the lighter fall out of his fingers, and down to the metal walkway.

"I've had *enough*," he seethed. "Enough of being told to 'sit' and 'play dead' and 'roll over.' They think we're too immature, well maybe we are. For all we know it's a good survival instinct. You two are proof of that."

Outside, the horde was even more frantic. Teeth gnashing. Nails scraping.

Vince cricked his neck as he sat up straighter. There was new swagger in his shoulders, like something had been reset. And setting fire to the photo was the final piece of the puzzle.

He looked out at the women. The murderers. The monsters. The zombies. "What you see is what you get," he shouted at them. "No more, no less. Take it or leave it, because as of today, I'm not putting up with this shit anymore."

From the woods, a monster in a traffic warden's uniform limped into view. She staggered over to the van, all claws and teeth, reaching out. There was something in her grasp. She slapped the window with it, and it stuck.

A parking ticket.

Vince stared at it. "For fuck's sake, really?"

He started the engine and turned on the headlights.

Neil looked around. "You do know the road's still blocked by the billboard, right?"

"Bollocks to the road," Vince muttered, shifting into gear. "I've been playing by the Highway Code my whole life and all it's got me is a one-way trip to Moodley. Hold on to something..."

He reached forward and turned on the radio. The speakers blared with the sound of wailing guitars, as Vince looked at his friends in the rearview. Cigar still between his teeth.

"...we're going off-road."

The wheels spun, flinging gravel behind them. The minibus lunged forward and rolled straight over the Traffic Warden, flattening her. A fistful of other tickets she held flittered off into the night.

The bus ploughed through the swarm. Monstrous zombies scattering in all directions, tumbling over the bonnet, slipping off the sides, falling under the wheels.

As he turned onto the street, he hit one after the other that came into view. He sped past the shops, with pedal to the metal.

By the church, the Zimmer Granny appeared hobbling across the street.

"Watch out for the old biddy!" Mikey shouted.

But it was too late.

What had once been a walking aid was now a weapon. She swung the frame like a club, slamming it into the windscreen with shocking force. The glass cracked on impact. Vince wrestled the wheel as the bus fishtailed, skidding wildly around the corner.

The bus sped over the curb and gardens.

Fences shattered. Garden gnomes went flying. Washing lines wrapped around side mirrors.

But the minibus didn't slow. Vince would not press the brake for anyone.

It hurtled forward, knocking down fence after fence, and crashing straight through the axe-ruined doghouse.

Mikey was barely able to keep a grip on his seat, as he was thrown around.

Neil clung to the front rail, enjoying every moment, until—

"Oh my God!"

There, lumbering into their path, arms wide like she meant to hug, was Bubbles.

She didn't last long.

The minibus hit her square on. And as the three-tonne vehicle hit, she exploded like a waterbed filled with lumpy soup. Fat, fluids, and other waste sprayed across the windscreen, dripping in through the cracks. Stinking.

The wipers engaged automatically. That just made it worse.

Mikey slid on his seat, barely upright. He saw nothing of what happened, but heard the disgusted reactions. "What was that?" he asked.

Neil and Vince answered in perfect deadpan: "Fat bird."

The final fence crumbled as the bus ran through it.

Beyond was the dark trees and tangled undergrowth of the woods. The woods they had been told not to go in.

Branches slapped the minibus' sides, as twigs shattered under the wheels. In front, in the glow of the headlights, shapes darted around, hundreds of them, but all too fast to see.

Vince expected an attack on the bus, but after a few hundred feet, the most shocking thing happened.

Good luck.

The road had returned.

With a shudder, the minibus sped back on to asphalt, and Vince shifted gears.

The minibus kept moving, cutting through the early light of dawn.

Somewhere deep underground, Graham woke with a start.

He was lying on a huge pile of corpses.

He was in the nest.

His gasps caught halfway, as his cracked ribs throbbed. He winced as he tried to sit up. Everything hurt. His ankle had been twisted to hell, and the rest of him looked like it had been used to sandpaper the floor. He was covered in grazes, cuts, gouges.

As he looked around the cave, he couldn't see any monsters. Not that he could see much in the dark. All that he *knew* was here, was death. He may not be able to see all the bodies, but he sure as hell could smell them. The stench hit him hard. He gagged uncontrollably.

He was alive.

He smiled in relief.

He then remembered the walkie-talkie still clipped to his belt. Its plastic was cracked but the thing still worked.

He unclipped it.

"Hello?" he spoke with a rasp.

Vince slammed on the brakes.

The tyres screamed across the road, leaving long, black lines of rubber behind them.

The music was switched off.

From the walkie-talkie came the voice again.

'Hello? Vince? Anyone there?'

Mikey was holding the walkie-talkie, staring at it, not knowing what to do.

Neil ran down the aisle and grabbed it off him. "Graham?" he said, almost laughing. "We thought you got squashed. Where are you?"

Graham's voice crackled back: *'I'm in the nest with all the stiffs. Where are you?'*

Vince got out of his seat and, without a word, took

the radio from Neil. He looked at the others. No dramatic pause, no speech. Just a look. The kind that said: *you know what we have to do.*

They nodded.

With a smirk, Vince spoke into the radio.

"Where are we?" he said. "We're coming to get you, you daft bastard."

The minibus spun to face the other way. Then it screamed its way back to Moodley.

Below, in the tunnels, Graham pulled himself off the pile of dead men. He couldn't walk properly, couldn't even think clearly, but he could move. And movement meant he wasn't dead yet. But he had to be as quiet as possible

He crawled over to the church tunnel as quickly as he could, but as he got close, the shadows around him moved.

He stopped and dropped like a stone back into the corpses.

It wasn't the two zombies that walked past him that nearly gave the game away. Not that one nearly smelled him, nor that one stood on his leg, causing him to hold his scream in. It was the dead body he had suddenly come face to face with.

Gavin, or what was left of his half-eaten corpse.

He was beyond dead, and now blankly stared out. Graham had to summon every piece of will power he had not to break down. He bit down on his own fist to keep from giving away his position.

Then he saw what Gavin still had in his hand. The Dolphin remote.

Slowly peering over his shoulder, Graham saw that the monsters were standing by the tunnel to the church, blocking his way. He'd have to find another way out... And there, behind the pile of bodies, another tunnel loomed, with a dull light coming from it.

The minibus rocketed past the Moodley sign again.

They were coming back to the place that nearly ate them.

Graham had made it to the new tunnel, without a monster seeing him.

He soon clambered to his feet, and limped away. Hoping he would find another staircase up. Any way out.

Ahead, a small generator room was lit by a single bulb. He grabbed the wire mesh gate for support as he got near, squinting at the wall of dusty modules and old cables.

A red sign read *DANGER: HIGH VOLTAGE* in bold letters. It sat above a new installation: a big metal box that had a dolphin logo stamped on it. A large switch sat next to it, and below that, a coiled power cable. More specifically, an unplugged power cable.

He quietly started to laugh.

. . .

"Hang on!" Vince yelled.

The minibus slammed into the remnants of the billboard, smashing through and clearing a path.

The wheels, though, didn't make it.

As the tires hit the broken wood they burst on impact. The rear axle also got caught and tore loose, dragging the shredded tyres away with it. Sparks flew from the undercarriage as the bus scraped and crunched to a halt on the car park.

Inside, the three slowly looked out of the windows.

"Okay, who's your favourite Spice Girl?" Neil said, pointing to down the high street.

Just outside the church, twenty of the Phase Two monsters stood. At the front, The Snipper. Beside her on either side, The Bride. The Butcher.

Vince turned from the window, lit with equal parts lunacy and bravery.

"Here's the plan," he said. "We get down there, have a bit of a ruck, pick up Graham, piss off to a pub somewhere nicer, and get shitfaced. Any questions?"

"Yeah," Mikey said. "Did you notice that we're slightly outnumbered?"

Vince held out his hand. "Pass me one of those clubs."

Mikey pulled a random club from Patrick's golf bag and handed it over. Vince looked at its tiny head and tossed it aside.

"Nah. Give me the sand wedge."

When it was passed over, it felt right.

Vince, cigar still smouldering, smiled as he rested the

wedge on his shoulder. "We're outnumbered and outgunned, but I've got the hump. So we're going to go out there in a very ungentlemanly fashion and, present company excepted, bash the living shit out of anything in a dress."

"Bloody hell, Vince," Neil said, vaguely horrified. "That's not very PC, is it?"

Vince and Mikey both looked at him in surprise.

They charged into the street like drunk extras in Braveheart. Golf clubs swinging, fists pumping, yelling incoherent threats as they ran.

Of course, they were parked at the car park and the horde was by the church, so it was a bit of a long run.

But when the monsters heard them approach, they acted with the same passion.

The whole of Moodley then seemed to shake as the two mobs ran down the street towards each other.

It was twenty against three. And beyond that twenty, hundreds more waited in the woods.

This was a final act of stupid defiance, and all three of them knew it,

But suddenly, the entire horde skidded to a halt, so abruptly that some nearly toppled over. Their frenzied charge stopped cold. They staggered and swayed but remained frozen in place.

A heavy silence fell, as thin trickles of blood began to leak from their ears.

The three slowed to a halt in front of the burned-out

toy shop, not quite sure if they were witnessing a miracle or a trap.

"Now what the fuck is that?" Neil asked.

"You think Phase Three's kicking in?" Vince asked, suspiciously.

"What's that gonna do?" Mikey replied. "Give them fucking wings?"

"Oi!" a voice rang out.

They turned to see Graham, dragging himself up the metal stairs from below the sandwich shop. Mud-caked, bloodied, limping, yet very much alive.

In his hand, he carried the Dolphin remote.

"I got it working," he said with pride, waving it in the air. "Some dickhead didn't even plug it in!"

They walked over, keeping an eye on the frozen horde, making sure they stayed in place.

On a nearby roof, a speaker sat. Though none of them could hear it, it was emitting a terrible noise not meant for their sex. And it was the same across the whole of Moodley, and out into the forest.

Neil snatched the remote from Graham's hand.

Without even thinking, he pressed the button.

The horde came to life. Suddenly snarling and running forward.

He pressed it again.

They came to a sudden stop once more. Frozen as the sound from the speakers started up again.

He laughed out loud. "Oh, this is bloody priceless."

He pressed it.

They advanced.

He pressed it again.

They stopped again.

Vince stared at the remote. "Remote controlled women. How perfect can it get?"

Neil grinned. "This is awesome.... Here, Vince. Have a go."

"Careful with it," Graham said, but Neil didn't listen to caution.

He tossed it over.

Vince went to catch it, but fumbled.

It slipped from his grasp and smashed against the pavement.

Cracking into pieces.

"Oops," Vince said, looking suddenly nervous.

"Bollocks." Neil added, turning to the horde.

The air changed, as every monstrous head turned.

By the now-cleared exit near the remains of the billboard, Graham was stuffed into the mini-mart trolley. Mikey, Vince and Neil ran, pushing him along. Laughing hysterically like West Ham supporters behind enemy lines at Millwall.

As they hit the road, they paused to look behind them.

From around the corner, a massive horde emerged. Hundreds of mutated Phase Two women, all the ones from the town as well as the woods, snarled and screamed for blood.

In the middle of the road, as they approached, the lads lined up.

Graham raised two fingers from the trolley.

Neil dropped his trousers and mooned them.

Mikey lifted his skirt and flashed his pants.

And Vince, fully reborn, stood dead centre, both middle fingers raised in defiance.

He was laughing harder than he had in years.

"And we freeze frame on that one last shot," Neil said, grinning from ear to ear.

Later...

"That's the story you wanna tell?" Mikey asked, taking a sip of his pint. "You don't think that the truth might be better? That we froze them in place and just ran like fuck?"

Neil shook his head, closing the script in front of him. "Artistic license, innit? Gotta have questions at the end. Will they make it? Won't they? Opens it up for a sequel."

Mikey looked confused. He peered at everyone else in the pub, then leaned in to ask his question, not wanting to be overheard. "Is this serious? You are really gonna try get this made?"

"Serious as soapy tits." Neil nodded. "You think I'd invite you mugs down the boozer to read this whole bloody thing for a laugh?"

"I gotta say," Graham said. "Thanks for keeping me gay."

"Yeah, but you didn't say I'm black," Mikey complained.

"Why would I?" Neil scoffed. "Didn't say I have brown eyes either, did I?"

"Uhh...I have a question," Patrick asked. "Why the fuck did you kill me off?"

"And me!" Matt added.

Banksy looked the most confused. "And you cut me out totally! I was right next to Patrick on that billboard. I was the one who found the dolphin remote."

"Lads, lads, lads," Neil said, his palms raised. "Calm your dicks... Yeah, I killed you. But it's all for the drama."

Banksy tutted. "Nah mate, it's a lie."

"Some of it was exaggerated, sure," Neil said, then held up his hand, still missing a little finger. "But there was a lot of truth in it too, right? I'd say 75% truth, 25% movie bollocks."

"Death by sword," Matt added. "At least I got a cool death."

"You are most welcome," Neil beamed.

Patrick grumbled. "You made me sound like a new age asshole, and a suicidal one at that!"

"Ah, it's not so bad," Vince said. "Sure, his story was... loose with the facts... And I did come off a bit sexist in places..." He glanced at Neil. "I mean you had me saying 'Fat bird'? Really?" He chuckled. "And not to mention that when I tell Ruth what you did to her, she'll string you up by your dick... But... none of that is important." He looked around the table and raised his glass. "We *all* survived Moodley. *That's* what matters...

We shouldn't be here... but we are. And Neil could sell this, we all get a cut... So... To us. To Lads F.C."

They all lifted their glasses. "Lads F.C."

"Wait," Matt said. "What is it gonna be called, this film? Gotta have a shit hot name, right?"

Neil's face brightened with a smile... "Oh, I got that one in the bag... The name... And you can just picture it in shiny lights on a marquee.... The name of our story is..." He leaned into Graham. "Drum roll, please, sir."

"Just say it!" Graham moaned trying not to laugh.

"The name is..." Neil laughed proudly. "ZOM-BIRDS!"

ECHO ON PUBLICATIONS

Official Novelizations
from Echo On Publication

In The Mouth
of Madness

Night of The Comet

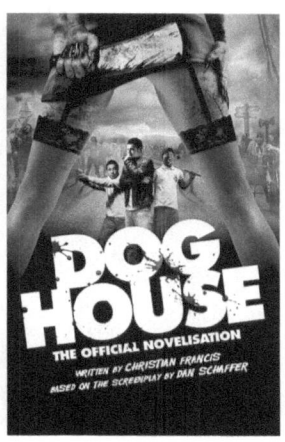

Doghouse

Witchboard

The Gate

The Descent
*In Partnership with
Titan Books*

check echohorror.com for more details

Official Novelizations
from Echo On Publication

Beneath Perfectiion
(Tremors)

Session 9

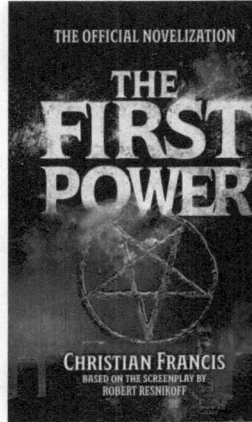

The First Power

Maniac Cop 1,2 & 3
*Avaialble individually or as a
collected hardcover*

**Dee Snider's
Strangeland**

**3615 Code
Santa Claus**

check echohorror.com for more details

Official Novelizations
Coming soon

WRONG TURN

SHOPPING

WAXWORK

XTRO

THE **DARK SIDE** OF THE **MOON**

NIGHTWISH

SPOOKIES

· **HOUSE** ·

FIDO

The **MONSTER SQUAD**

DRACULA 2000

check echohorror.com for more details

Original Novels and Novellas
by Christian Francis

The Dead Woods
YA Horror

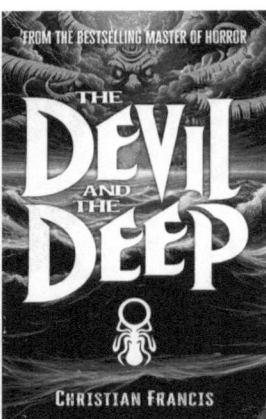

**The Devil
and The Deep**
Cosmic Horror

**The Sacrifice of
Anton Stacey**
Horror Novella

The Animus Chronicles Part 1
Everyday Monsters
Horror/Dark Fantasy

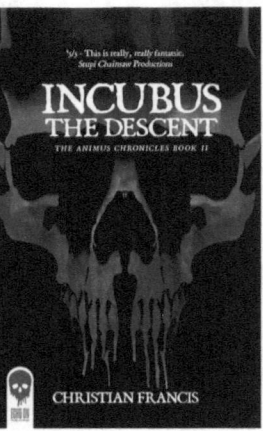

The Animus Chronicles Part 2
Incubus: The Descent
Horror/Dark Fantasy

www.ingramcontent.com/pod-product-compliance
Lightning Source LLC
Chambersburg PA
CBHW060546190726
48283CB00003B/893